DISTANT STAR

Also by Roberto Bolaño in English translation

BY NIGHT IN CHILE

Roberto Bolaño

DISTANT STAR

Translated from the Spanish by
Chris Andrews

THE HARVILL PRESS
LONDON

First published with the title *Estrella distante* by
Editorial Anagrama, S.A., 1996

2 4 6 8 10 9 7 5 3 1

Copyright © The Estate of Roberto Bolaño and Editorial Anagrama, S.A.
English translation © Chris Andrews, 2004

Roberto Bolaño has asserted his right under the Copyright, Designs and patents Act 1988 to
be identified as the author of this work

This edition has been translated with the financial assistance of the
Spanish Dirección General del Libro y Bibliotecas, Ministerio de Cultura

First published in Great Britain in 2004 by
The Harvill Press
Random House, 20 Vauxhall Bridge Road,
London SWIV 2SA

Random House Australia (Pty) Limited
20 Alfred Street, Milsons Point, Sydney,
New South Wales 2061, Australia

Random House New Zealand Limited
18 Poland Road, Glenfield,
Auckland 10, New Zealand

Random House South Africa (Pty) Limited
Endulini, 5A Jubilee Road, Parktown 2193, South Africa

The Random House Group Limited Reg. No 954009
www.randomhouse.co.uk/harvill

A CIP catalogue record for this book
is available from the British Library

ISBN 1 8434 3094 0

Papers used by Random House are natural,
recyclable products made from wood grown in sustainable forests;
the manufacturing processes conform to the environmental
regulations of the country of origin

Typeset in Adobe Garamond by Palimpsest Book Production Limited,
Polmont, Stirlingshire

Printed and bound in Great Britain
by Mackays of Chatham plc

For Victoria Ávalos and Lautaro Bolaño

"What star falls unseen?"
WILLIAM FAULKNER

In the final chapter of my novel Nazi Literature in America *I recounted, in less than twenty pages and perhaps too schematically, the story of Lieutenant Ramírez Hoffman of the Chilean Air Force, which I heard from a fellow Chilean, Arturo B., a veteran of Latin America's doomed revolutions, who tried to get himself killed in Africa. He was not satisfied with my version. It was meant to counterbalance the preceding excursions into the literary grotesque, or perhaps to come as an anticlimax, and Arturo would have preferred a longer story that, rather than mirroring or exploding others, was, in itself, a mirror and an explosion. So we took that final chapter and shut ourselves up for a month and a half in my house in Blanes, where, guided by his dreams and nightmares, we composed the present novel. My role was limited to preparing refreshments, consulting a few books, and discussing the reuse of numerous paragraphs with Arturo and the increasingly animated ghost of Pierre Ménard.*

I

I saw Carlos Wieder for the first time in 1971, or perhaps in 1972, when Salvador Allende was President of Chile.

At that stage Wieder was calling himself Alberto Ruiz-Tagle and occasionally attended Juan Stein's poetry workshop in Concepción, the so-called capital of the South. I can't say I knew him well. I saw him once or twice a week at the workshop. He wasn't particularly talkative. I was. Most of us there talked a lot, not just about poetry, but politics, travel (little did we know what our travels would be like), painting, architecture, photography, revolution and the armed struggle that would usher in a new life and a new era, so we thought, but which, for most of us, was like a dream, or rather the key that would open the door into a world of dreams, the only dreams worth living for. And even though we were vaguely aware that dreams often turn into nightmares, we didn't let that bother us. Our ages ranged from seventeen to twenty-three (I was eighteen) and most of us were students in the Faculty of Literature, except the Garmendia sisters, who were studying sociology and psychology, and Alberto Ruiz-Tagle, who, as he said at some point, was an autodidact. What this meant in Chile in the years before 1973 is in itself an interesting subject. But to tell the truth, he didn't strike me as an autodidact. What I mean is: he didn't *look* like one. In Chile, at the beginning of the seventies, autodidacts didn't dress like Ruiz-Tagle. They were poor. True, he talked like an autodidact. I guess he talked the way we all do now, those of us who are still alive (he talked as if he were living inside a cloud), but I couldn't believe, from the way he dressed, that he had never set foot in a university. I don't mean he was a dandy – although, in his own way, he was – or that he dressed in a particular style. His tastes were eclectic: sometimes he would turn up in a suit and tie; other days he'd be wearing sports gear, and he wasn't averse to jeans and T-shirts. But whatever he was wearing, it was always an expensive brand. In other words, Ruiz-Tagle was well dressed, and in those days, in Chile, autodidacts were too busy steering a course between lunacy and destitution to dress like that, or so I thought. He once said that his father or his grandfather used to have an estate near Puerto Montt. At the age of fifteen he had decided, so he told us, or perhaps we heard it from Veronica Garmendia, to quit school and devote himself to working on the property and reading the books in his father's library. At Juan Stein's poetry workshop we all assumed he was a skilled horseman. I don't know why, because we never saw him ride. In fact, all our suppositions concerning Ruiz-Tagle were predetermined by our jealousy or perhaps our envy. He was tall and slim, but well built and handsome. According to Bibiano O'Ryan, his face was too inexpressive to be handsome, but of course he said

4

this with the benefit of hindsight, so it hardly counts. Why were we jealous of Ruiz-Tagle? The plural is misleading. *I* was jealous of him. Bibiano too perhaps. Why? Because of the Garmendia sisters, naturally: identical twins and the undisputed stars of the poetry workshop. In fact we sometimes felt, Bibiano and I, that Stein was running the workshop for their benefit alone. I have to admit they outshone us all. Veronica and Angelica Garmendia: so alike some days it was impossible to tell them apart, yet other days (and especially other *nights*) so different that they seemed to be strangers to each other, if not enemies. Stein adored them. Along with Ruiz-Tagle, he was the only one who always knew which twin was which. It's not easy for me to talk about them. Sometimes they appear in my nightmares: the same age as I was, or perhaps a year older, tall, slim, with dark skin and black hair, very long black hair – it was the fashion back then, I think.

The Garmendia sisters made friends with Ruiz-Tagle almost straight away. He enrolled in Stein's workshop in '71 or '72. No-one had seen him before, at the university or anywhere else. Stein didn't inquire where he was from. He asked him to read out three poems and said they weren't bad. (The only poems he ever praised without reserve were those of the Garmendia sisters.) And that was how Ruiz-Tagle joined our group. At first the rest of us didn't pay him much attention. But when we saw that the Garmendia sisters were making friends with him, we did too. Up until then he had been affable but distant. Only with the Garmendia girls (and in this he resembled Stein) was he positively friendly, unfailingly kind and attentive. With the rest of us he was, as I said, affable but distant, by which I mean that he would greet us with a smile; when we read out our poems, he was discreet and measured in his critical judgments; he never defended his work against our generally devastating attacks, and when we talked, he listened in a manner that I certainly wouldn't describe as attentive now, although that is how it seemed to us then.

The differences between Ruiz-Tagle and the rest of us were obvious. We spoke a sort of slang or jargon derived in equal parts from Marx and Mandrake the Magician (we were mostly members or sympathisers of the MIR or Trotskyist parties, although a few of us belonged to the Young Socialists or the Communist Party or one of the leftist Catholic parties), while Ruiz-Tagle spoke Spanish, the Spanish of certain parts of Chile (mental rather than physical regions) where time seems to have come to a standstill. We lived with our parents (those of us who were from Concepción) or in spartan student boarding-houses; Ruiz-Tagle lived on his own, in a flat near the centre of town, with four rooms and the curtains permanently drawn. I never visited this flat, but many years later Bibiano O'Ryan told me about it, no doubt under the influence of the sinister legend that had grown up around Wieder, so I don't know how much to believe and how much to put down to my fellow student's imagination. We hardly ever had two dimes to rub together (it seems so odd to be writing the word *dime*: I can see it shining like an eye in the night); Ruiz-Tagle was never short of money.

What did Bibiano say about Ruiz-Tagle's flat? He talked about how bare it was, mostly; he had the feeling it had been *prepared.* He only went there once on his own. He was passing by and, typically, decided to drop in and invite Ruiz-Tagle to go and see a film. He hardly knew the guy, but that didn't stop him. There was a Bergman film showing, I can't remember which one. Bibiano had already been to the flat a couple of times with one or other of the Garmendia sisters, and on both occasions the visit had been expected, so to speak. Both times, the flat seemed to have been *prepared,* its contents arranged for the eye of the imminent visitor; it was too empty, and there were spaces from which things had obviously been removed. In the letter explaining all this to me (which was written many years later), Bibiano said he felt like Mia Farrow in *Rosemary's Baby,* when she goes into the neighbour's house for the first time with John Cassavettes. What was missing from Ruiz-Tagle's flat was something unnameable (or something that Bibiano, years later, and knowing the full story, or a good part of it at any rate, considered unnameable, but palpably present), as if the host had amputated parts of the interior. Or as if the interior were a kind of Meccano that could be reconstructed to fit the expectations and particularities of each visitor. The impression was even stronger when he visited the flat on his own. This time, of course, Ruiz-Tagle, had not been expecting him. He took a long time to open the door. And then he seemed not to recognize his visitor, although Bibiano assured me that he came to the door with a smile and went on smiling throughout what followed. There was not much light, as Bibiano himself admitted in his letter, so I don't know quite how accurate my friend's account is. In any case, Ruiz-Tagle opened the door, and after

7

a rather incongruous exchange (at first he didn't understand that Bibiano was proposing they go and see a film), he asked him to wait a moment, shut the door, opened it again after a few seconds, and invited him in. The flat was dimly lit. The air was thick with a peculiar odour, as if Ruiz-Tagle had cooked something very pungent the night before, something oily and spicy. For a moment, Bibiano thought he heard a noise in one of the rooms and assumed there was a woman in the flat. He was about to excuse himself and leave when Ruiz-Tagle asked which film he was thinking of going to see. Bibiano said a Bergman film, at the Teatro Lautaro. Ruiz-Tagle kept wearing that smile of his, which, according to Bibiano was enigmatic, but which always struck me as self-satisfied if not downright arrogant. He excused himself, saying he already had a date with Veronica Garmendia; and anyway, he explained, he didn't like Bergman's films. By that stage, Bibiano was sure there was someone else in the flat, hiding behind a door and listening to the conversation. He thought it must have been Veronica; otherwise why would Ruiz-Tagle, who was normally so discreet, have mentioned her name? But try as he might, he couldn't imagine our star poet in that situation. Neither Veronica nor Angelica Garmendia would stoop to eavesdropping. So who was it? Bibiano never found out. Right then, probably the only thing he knew was that he wanted to get out of there, away from Ruiz-Tagle, and never return to that naked, bleeding flat. Those are his words. Although, to judge from his description, the flat could not have looked more antiseptic. Clean walls, books lined up on the metal shelves, armchairs covered with Mapuche ponchos,

Ruiz-Tagle's Leica sitting on a wooden bench (he brought it to the poetry workshop one afternoon to take photos of us all). The kitchen door was ajar and Bibiano could see in: it looked normal, except that there were no piles of dirty plates, none of the mess you'd expect in the flat of a student who lives on his own (but then Ruiz-Tagle wasn't a student). In short, nothing out of the ordinary, except for the noise, which could easily have come from the flat next door. While Ruiz-Tagle was talking, Bibiano had the distinct impression that his host didn't want him to leave and was prolonging the conversation precisely to keep him there. Although there was no objective basis for this impression, it contributed to my friend's nervous agitation, which soon reached a degree he described as intolerable. The strange thing is that Ruiz-Tagle seemed to be enjoying himself: he could see Bibiano growing paler and sweating more profusely, yet he went on talking (about Bergman, presumably), smiling all the while. Rather than breaking the close silence of the flat, his words accentuated it.

What exactly did Ruiz-Tagle say? It might be important, if only I could remember, Bibiano wrote in his letter, but however hard I try, I can't. In any case, he stayed until he couldn't bear it any more, then rather brusquely he said, See you later, and left. At the bottom of the stairs, he ran into Veronica Garmendia. She asked what had happened to him. What do you mean? Why should anything have happened to me? asked Bibiano. I don't know, said Veronica, but you're as white as a sheet. I'll never forget her saying that, wrote Bibiano: *white as a sheet*. And Veronica Garmendia's face. The face of a woman in love.

9

It's hard to admit, but it's true. Veronica was in love with Ruiz-Tagle. And it's possible that Angelica was in love with him too. We talked about it once, Bibiano and I, a long time ago. I suppose we were miserable because neither of the girls was in love with us, or even paid us much attention. Bibiano liked Veronica, while I preferred Angelica. We never dared declare our feelings, although I suppose they were common knowledge. And in this respect we were no different from the other young men at the workshop, all of whom were more or less in love with the Garmendia sisters. But the twins, or one of them at least, had succumbed to the peculiar charm of the poetry-writing autodidact.

He may have been an autodidact, but he was keen to learn, as Bibiano and I discovered when he appeared at the University of Concepción's rival poetry workshop, run by Diego Soto, whose approach differed markedly from that of Stein in ethical as well as aesthetic matters, although the two were what used to be, and I suppose still are, called soul mates. For some reason, Soto's workshop was held in the Faculty of Medicine, in a poorly ventilated, poorly furnished room, just across the corridor from the theatre where the anatomy students used to dissect corpses. The theatre smelt of formalin, of course. Sometimes the corridor smelt of formalin too. And some nights – Soto's workshop was held every Friday night from eight to ten, although it usually finished after midnight – the smell of formalin infiltrated our room, and we tried in vain to smother it, smoking cigarette after cigarette. The regulars at Stein's workshop didn't attend Soto's and vice versa, except for Bibiano

O'Ryan and myself. We made up for skipping almost all our classes by attending not only both workshops, but also every reading and cultural or political event that was held in the city. So when we saw Ruiz-Tagle turn up one night at Soto's workshop it was a surprise. He behaved more or less as he did at Stein's. He listened; his critical remarks were thoughtful, brief and always proffered in a polite and well-meaning manner. He read his own work with a certain disengagement and distance, and accepted even the harshest comments without protest, as if the poems he had submitted for our criticism were not his own. Bibiano and I were not the only ones to notice this; one night Diego Soto told him that there was something distant and cold about his writing. It's as if they weren't your poems, he said. Ruiz-Tagle nodded in agreement. I'm still trying to find my voice, he said.

At the workshop in the Faculty of Medicine, Ruiz-Tagle got to know Carmen Villagrán and they became friends. Carmen was a good poet, although not as good as the Garmendia sisters. (The best poets or potential poets went to Juan Stein's workshop.) He also met and befriended Marta Posadas, known as Fat Marta, the only medical student who attended the workshop in the Faculty of Medicine: a very white, very fat, very sad girl who wrote prose poems and cherished the dream, back then at least, of becoming the Marta Harnecker of Chilean literary criticism.

Ruiz-Tagle didn't make any friends among the male poets. When he saw Bibiano and me, he greeted us politely but without showing the slightest sign of familiarity, in spite of the fact that, because of the two poetry workshops, we were spending eight or nine hours in his company each week. He seemed to be indifferent to men in general. He lived on his own; there was something strange about his flat (according to Bibiano); he was devoid of the puerile pride that most poets take in their work, and not only was he friends with the most beautiful girls of my generation (the Garmendia sisters), he had also conquered the hearts of the two women in Diego Soto's workshop. He was, in a word, the focus of Bibiano's envy, and of mine.

And nobody really knew him.

Juan Stein and Diego Soto, who for Bibiano and me were the two most intelligent people in Concepción, had no idea about him. Nor did the Garmendia sisters. In fact, on two occasions Angelica sang the praises of Ruiz-Tagle in my presence: he was serious, well mannered, a clear thinker, and a very good listener. Bibiano and I hated him, but we had no idea either. Fat Marta was the only one who glimpsed a part of what was lurking behind the façade. I remember the night we talked about him. The three of us had been to the cinema and after the film we went to a restaurant in the centre of town. Bibiano was making his eleventh bid to publish a short anthology of work by Concepción's young poets in one of the local newspapers, and had brought along a folder with contributions from the members of Stein's and Soto's workshops. Fat Marta and I started going through the poems. Who are you going to include? I asked, knowing full well that I was among the chosen. (Had I not been, my friendship with Bibiano would probably have come to an end the next day.) You, said Bibiano, Martita (Fat

Marta), Veronica and Angelica, of course, Carmen. Then he mentioned two other poets, one from Stein's workshop, the other from Soto's, and finally he pronounced the name Ruiz-Tagle. I remember Marta said nothing for a moment while her fingers (which were permanently ink stained, the nails not very clean either – surprising for a medical student, though it was obvious from the lethargic way she talked about her course that she would never complete it) scrabbled through the papers until she found Ruiz-Tagle's three sheets. Don't put him in, she said suddenly. You mean Ruiz-Tagle? I asked. I couldn't believe my ears: she was one of his most fervent admirers. Bibiano, meanwhile, said nothing. The three poems were short; all less than ten lines. One described a landscape: trees, a dirt road, a house in the distance, wooden fences, hills, clouds. According to Bibiano it was "very Japanese". I thought it was like something Jorge Teillier might have written after suffering a stroke. The second poem (which was entitled "Air") was about wind blowing through the gaps in the stone walls of a house. (This one sounded like Teillier stricken with aphasia but persevering in his literary endeavours, a style that should not have been totally unfamiliar to me, since even back then, in 1973, at least half of Teillier's putative disciples were persevering, undaunted by aphasia.) I have forgotten the third poem altogether. Or almost: I remember that at some point in it a knife appeared, for a reason that remained entirely obscure to me.

Why don't you think I should include him? asked Bibiano, slumped forward, with his head resting on his outstretched arm as if it were a pillow and the table were his bed. I thought you were friends, I said. We are, said Fat Marta, but I still wouldn't put him in. Why not? insisted Bibiano. Fat Marta shrugged. Then she said, It's as if they weren't his poems. His real poems, if you see what I mean. What *do* you mean? asked Bibiano. Marta looked me in the eye (I was sitting opposite, and Bibiano, beside her, seemed to have fallen asleep) and said, Alberto is a good poet, but he still hasn't made his breakthrough. You mean he's a virgin? asked Bibiano, but Fat Marta and I ignored him. Have you read other poems of his? I inquired. What does he write? What's it like? Fat Marta smiled inwardly, as if she herself couldn't believe what she was about to tell us. Alberto, she said, is going to revolutionize Chilean poetry. Have you actually read his stuff, or is this just a feeling you have? Fat Marta gave a little snort by way of reply. Then, abruptly, she said, The other day I went to his flat. We didn't tell her to go on, but I noticed that Bibiano, slumped on the table, was smiling at her affectionately. He wasn't expecting me, of course, she added. I know what you're trying to tell us, said Bibiano. Alberto opened up to me, said Fat Marta. I can't imagine Ruiz-Tagle opening up to anybody, said Bibiano. Everyone thinks he's in love with Veronica Garmendia, said Marta, but it's not true. Is that what he told you? asked Bibiano. Fat Marta smiled to herself, as if she were in possession of a great secret. At that point I remember thinking, I don't like this woman. She might be talented, she might be intelligent, she's on the right side, but I don't like her. No, he didn't tell me that, said Marta, although he tells me things he doesn't tell anyone else. You mean, he doesn't tell other *girls*, said Bibiano. Right, she said, things he doesn't tell the other girls. Things like what? Fat Marta thought for a while before answering. Well, he tells me about his new poetry, what else? You mean the poetry he's planning to write? asked Bibiano sceptically. That he's going to *perform*, said Marta. And you know why I'm so sure? Because of his will. She waited a moment for a question from us, then added, He has a will of iron. You don't know him. It was late. Bibiano looked at Fat Marta and got up to pay. If you've got so much faith in him, how come you don't want Bibiano to put him in the anthology? I asked. We wrapped our scarves around our necks (never since have I worn a scarf as long as the ones we had then) and went out into the cold street. Because they're not *his* poems, said Marta. And how do you know? I asked with mounting irritation. Because I can read people, she said sadly, looking at the empty street. How conceited can you get, I thought. Bibiano was the last out of the door. Martita, he said, there are not many things I'm sure about, but one of them is that Ruiz-Tagle is not going to revolutionise Chilean poetry. I don't think he's even a socialist, I added. Surprisingly, Marta agreed with me. No, he's not, she said, her voice sounding even sadder. For a moment I thought she was going to burst into tears and I tried to change the subject. Bibiano laughed. With friends like you, she said, who needs enemies? Bibiano hadn't meant to be cruel, of course, but she was hurt and tried to storm off. We accompanied her home. In the bus we talked about the film and the political situation. Before saying good-night, she looked at us fixedly and said she had to ask us to promise her something. What? asked Bibiano. What we were talking about, don't mention it to

Alberto. O.K., said Bibiano, I promise, we won't say you didn't want him in my anthology. It's not as if anyone's going to publish it, said Fat Marta. Probably not, he admitted. Thanks, Bibi, she said (nobody else ever called him that) and gave him a peck on the cheek. We won't tell him anything, I swear, I said. Thanks, thanks, thanks, said Marta. I thought she was joking. Don't say anything to Veronica either, she said. She could tell Alberto and then, you know . . . No, we won't tell her. Promise it won't go beyond us three, said Marta. We promised. Finally Fat Marta turned away, opened the door of her building and we saw her get into the lift. Before disappearing, she waved to us one last time. What a peculiar woman, said Bibiano. I laughed. We walked back to our respective places of residence: he to his boarding house and I to the family home. Chilean poetry, said Bibiano that night, isn't going to change until we learn how to read Enrique Lihn properly. In other words, not for a long time.

A few days later the army seized power and the government collapsed.

One night I rang the Garmendia sisters, for no particular reason, just to see how they were. We're leaving, said Veronica. With a lump in my throat I asked when. Tomorrow. In spite of the curfew, I insisted on going over. The flat where the two of them lived was not too far from my house and, besides, it wasn't the first time I had broken the curfew. It was 10.00 by the time I arrived. To my surprise, they were drinking tea and reading (I guess I had expected to find them hatching escape plans amid a chaos of half-packed cases). They weren't leaving the country, they told me, but moving to their parents' house in Nacimiento, a town a few kilometres from Concepción. What a relief, I said, I thought you were going to Sweden or somewhere like that. If only, said Angelica. Then we talked about the friends we hadn't seen for a few days and launched into the inevitable speculations: who was under arrest for sure, who might have gone into hiding, who was being hunted. The sisters were not afraid (they had no reason to be; they were only students, and apart from being friends with a few activists, mainly from the Faculty of Sociology, they had no links with the so-called "extremists"), but they were going to Nacimiento because Concepción had become unbearable and, as they admitted, they always went back to the family home when "real life" revealed its deeply unpleasant bent for the ugly and the brutal. Well, you better go right away, I said, because it looks like we're hosting the world championship in ugliness and brutality. They laughed and told me to go home. I insisted on staying a little longer. I remember that night as one of the happiest of my life. At 1.00 in the morning Veronica said I might as well stay. None of us had eaten, so we crammed into the kitchen and improvised a little feast of scrambled eggs, fried onions, fresh-baked bread and tea. Suddenly I felt happy, immensely happy, capable of anything, although I was aware that meanwhile all that I believed in was collapsing for ever, and that many people, several friends of mine among them, were being hunted down or tortured. But I felt like singing and dancing, and the bad news (or the depressing commentaries on the bad news) only added fuel to the fire of my joy, to use an expression which is, I admit, impossibly trite ("corny" we would have said back then) but does convey how I (and I dare say the Garmendia sisters) felt, along with many other Chileans who, in September 1973, had not yet reached the age of twenty-one.

At 5.00 in the morning I fell asleep on the sofa. Angelica woke me four hours later. We had breakfast in the kitchen, in silence. At midday, they put a pair of suitcases in their car, a lime-green '68 model Citroneta and left for Nacimiento. I never saw them again.

Their parents, both painters, had died before the twins' fifteenth birthday, in a car accident, I think. I once saw a photograph of them: he was dark and lean with very prominent cheekbones and a certain look of sadness and perplexity peculiar to those born south of the river Bío-Bío; she was or seemed to be taller than him, slightly chubby, with a sweet, easy-going smile.

When they died, their daughters inherited the house in Nacimiento – a three-storey place (the top storey was one big attic room, which the parents had used as a studio) built of stone and wood, on the outskirts of town – as well as some land near Mulchén, which provided the girls with a comfortable living. They often talked about their parents (according to them, Julián Garmendia was one of the best painters of his generation, although I have never heard or seen him mentioned anywhere) and their poems often described painters lost in the wilds of southern Chile, embarking on hopelessly ambitious works and hopelessly in love. Is that how Julián Garmendia loved María Oyarzún? I find it hard to believe when I think of that photo. But I don't find it hard to believe that in the 1960s, in Chile, there were people who were hopelessly in love. It seems strange to me now. Like a film misplaced on a forgotten shelf in some enormous archive. But I don't doubt it for a moment.

From here on, my story is mainly conjecture. The Garmendia sisters went to Nacimiento, to their big house on the outskirts of town where their mother's older sister, a certain Ema Oyarzún, lived together with an elderly maid, Amalia Maluenda.

They went to Nacimiento and shut themselves up in the house, and one fine day, say two weeks or a month later (although I doubt a month had gone by), Alberto Ruiz-Tagle turned up on their doorstep.

It must have happened something like this. One afternoon, one of those bracing yet melancholic southern afternoons, a car appears on the dirt road, but the twins don't hear, because they're playing the piano or busy in the orchard or stacking firewood at the back of the house with their aunt and the maid. Someone knocks at the front door. Knocks and knocks and finally the maid opens the door and there is Ruiz-Tagle. He says he has come to see the twins. The maid doesn't let him in and says she will go and call the girls. Ruiz-Tagle waits patiently, seated in a cane armchair on the broad porch. When the twins see him, they greet him effusively and scold the maid for not having shown him in. For the first half-hour, Ruiz-Tagle is bombarded with questions. No doubt he strikes the aunt as a pleasant young man: nice-looking, polite. The twins are happy. Ruiz-Tagle is invited to dinner, of course, and in his honour they prepare a feast. I don't want to think about what they might have eaten. Corn-cakes perhaps or *empanadas*, but no, it must have been something else. Naturally, they invite him to spend the night. Ruiz-Tagle accepts without a fuss. After dinner they stay up late talking, and the twins read some poems: the aunt in raptures, Ruiz-Tagle knowing and silent. He, of course, doesn't read anything; he says that after poems like theirs, his don't rate. The aunt insists, Please, Alberto, read us something of yours, but he will not be moved. He says he has nearly finished something new, but until it is finished and corrected, he would prefer not to talk about it. He smiles, shrugs, says, No, sorry, no, no, no, and the twins take his side, Leave him alone, Aunty. In their innocence they *think* they understand, but they don't understand at all (the "New Chilean Poetry" is about to be born), and yet they think they understand and they read their poems, their wonderful poems, while Ruiz-Tagle looks on, smiling (and no doubt closing his eyes the better to listen), and the aunt is occasionally offended or perplexed: Angelica, how can you be so crude? Or, Veronica, dear, I didn't understand a thing. Alberto, can you explain that metaphor to me? And Ruiz-Tagle politely obliging, talking about signifier and signified, about Joyce Mansour, Sylvia Plath and Alejandra Pizarnik (although the twins say, No, no, we don't like Pizarnik, by which they really mean that they don't *write* like Pizarnik), and the aunt nodding attentively as Ruiz-Tagle goes on to mention Violeta and Nicanor Parra (I met Violeta, in her tent, I did, says poor Ema Oyarzún), and then Enrique Lihn and "civil poetry", and here if the twins were more attentive they would have seen an ironic glint in his eye (civil poetry, I'll give you civil poetry), and finally, in full flight now, he starts talking about Jorge Cáceres, the Chilean surrealist who died in 1949 at the age of twenty-six.

And then the twins get up, or perhaps it's only Veronica who goes to look in her father's sizeable library and returns with a book by Cáceres, *Bound for the Great Polar Pyramid*, published when the poet was only twenty. From time to time the Garmendia sisters, or maybe it was only Angelica, used to talk about republishing the complete works of Cáceres, a legendary figure for our generation, so it's not surprising that Ruiz-Tagle brings him up (although he has nothing to do with the sisters' poetry; Violeta Parra does, Nicanor too, but not Cáceres). He also mentions Anne Sexton and Elizabeth Bishop and Denise Levertov (poets whose work the twins adore and have on occasion translated and read at the workshop, to the evident satisfaction of Juan Stein) and then they all make fun of the aunt, who doesn't understand anything, and they eat home-made biscuits and play the guitar and someone notices the maid, who has been standing in the corridor, watching them from the shadows, not daring to come in, and the aunt says, Come on, Amalia, don't stand there like a waif, and the maid, drawn by the music and the revelry, takes two steps forward, but no more, and then night falls and the party is over.

A few hours later Alberto Ruiz-Tagle, although from here on I should call him Carlos Wieder, gets up.

Everyone is asleep. He has probably slept with Veronica Garmendia. It's not important. (What I mean is: not any more; at the time, of course, it was, unfortunately for us.) At any rate,

Carlos Wieder gets up like a sleepwalker, without hesitation, and quietly searches the house. He is looking for the aunt's bedroom. His shadow moves over the paintings by Julián Garmendia and María Oyarzún that line the corridors, along with plates and dishes from the area around Nacimiento (which is famous, I believe, for its china or pottery). Wieder stealthily opens door after door. Finally he finds the aunt's room, on the ground floor, next to the kitchen. The room opposite is sure to be the maid's. And as he slips in to the aunt's room he hears the sound of a car approaching the house. He smiles; no time to lose. In a bound he is beside the bed. In his right hand, he holds a curved knife. Ema Oyarzún is sleeping placidly. Wieder takes the pillow and covers her face with it. Straight away, with a single stroke of the knife, he cuts her throat. The car pulls up in front of the house. Wieder has already left the aunt's room and is going into the maid's. But the bed is empty. For a moment Wieder doesn't know what to do; he is seized by a desire to kick the bed, smash up the rickety old chest of drawers in which Amalia Maluenda's clothes are piled. But it lasts only a moment. Soon he is at the front door, breathing normally, letting in the four men who came in the car. They greet him with a discreet but respectful nod and peer obscenely at the dark interior, the carpets, the curtains, as if from the very start they were searching out and weighing up places to hide. But they are not the ones who will be hiding.

With these men the night comes into the Garmendias' house. Fifteen minutes later, or ten perhaps, when they leave, the night leaves with them. The night comes in, and out it goes again, swift and efficient. And the bodies will never be found; but no, *one* body, just one, will appear years later in a mass grave, the body of Angelica Garmendia, my adorable, my incomparable Angelica, but only hers, as if to prove that Carlos Wieder is a man and not a god.

2

Around that time, as the last life rafts of the Popular Unity Front were sinking, I was taken prisoner. The circumstances of my arrest were banal, if not grotesque, but being imprisoned, rather than hanging around in the street or in a café or, more likely, holed up in my room refusing to get out of bed, meant that I witnessed Carlos Wieder's first poetic act, although at that stage I didn't know who Carlos Wieder was or what had befallen the Garmendia sisters.

It happened late one afternoon – Wieder was fond of twilight – while the prisoners, about seventy of us, were killing time at La Peña, a transit centre on the outskirts of Concepción, practically in Talcahuano, playing chess in the yard or just talking.

A few strands of cloud appeared in the sky, which half an hour earlier had been absolutely clear. Drifting east, shaped like cigarettes or pencils, the clouds were black and white at first, when they were still over the coast, but as they veered towards the city they turned pink, then bright vermilion as they headed up the valley.

For some reason I had the impression I was the only prisoner looking at the sky. It might have had something to do with being nineteen years old.

Then, among the clouds, the aeroplane appeared. At first it was a spot no bigger than a mosquito. I thought it must have come from an airstrip somewhere nearby and be returning to base after a flight along the coast. It approached the city slowly but steadily, as if it were gliding, hard to make out among the strips of high cirrus and the pencil-shaped clouds trailed by the wind just above the rooftops.

It seemed to be moving as slowly as the clouds, but that, I soon realised, was an optical illusion. When it flew over the transit centre, it made a noise like a damaged washing-machine. The pilot's face was visible, and for a moment I thought I saw him raise his hand and wave us good-bye. Then the plane turned its nose up and climbed, and soon it was flying over the centre of Concepción.

There, high above the city, it began to write a poem in the sky. At first I thought the pilot had gone mad and I wasn't surprised. Madness was not exceptional at the time. I thought he was looping around in a fit of desperation and would crash into a building or a square in the city. But then, suddenly, the letters appeared, as if the sky itself had secreted them. Perfectly formed letters of grey-black smoke on the sky's enormous screen of rose-tinged blue, chilling the eyes of those who saw them. IN PRINCIPIO . . . CREAVIT DEUS . . . CAELUM ET TERRAM, I read as if in a dream. I supposed – or hoped – it was part of an advertising campaign. I chuckled to myself. Then the plane swung around and flew west, heading towards us, before turning again to make another pass. This time the line of words was much longer and it stretched out over the southern suburbs. TERRA AUTEM ERAT INANIS . . . ET VACUA . . . ET TENEBRAE ERANT . . . SUPER FACIEM ABYSSI . . . ET SPIRITUS DEI . . . FEREBATUR SUPER AQUAS . . .

For a moment it seemed the plane would disappear over the horizon, heading for the coastal range or the Andes, one or the other, I really couldn't tell, heading south anyway, towards the great forests. But it came back.

By then almost everyone in the city centre was watching the sky. One of the prisoners, a man called Norberto, who was going mad (or such, at least, was the diagnosis pronounced by a fellow prisoner, a socialist psychiatrist who was later executed, so I heard, in full possession of his intellectual and emotional faculties), tried to climb the fence that separated the men's yard from the women's, and started shouting, It's a Messerschmitt 109, a Messerschmitt fighter from the Luftwaffe, the best fighter plane of 1940! I stared at him and then at the rest of the prisoners, and everything seemed to be immersed in a transparent grey wash, as if the La Peña Centre were dissolving in time. The pair of guards at the entrance to the gymnasium, where we slept on the floor, had stopped talking and were looking at the sky. So were all the prisoners, who had risen to their feet, abandoning their games of chess, their confessions, their speculations on the days ahead and what they held in store. Clinging to the fence like a monkey, Mad Norberto laughed and said, The Second World War is returning to the Earth. All that talk about the Third World War was wrong; it's the Second returning, returning, returning. And it has fallen to us, the people of Chile, to greet and welcome it – Oh lucky day! he cried, as the white froth of his saliva, contrasting with the dominant tone of grey, ran down his chin, dripped onto the collar of his shirt and spread out in a large wet patch on his chest.

The plane veered around and came back over the centre of Concepción. I managed to read the words DIXITQUE DEUS . . . FIAT LUX . . . ET FACTA EST LUX, though perhaps I was guessing or imagining or dreaming. The women on the other side of the fence were shading their eyes with their hands and following the plane's loops attentively like us, but in heart-rending silence. For a moment I thought that if Norberto had tried to jump the fence, no-one would have stopped him. All the other prisoners and guards were frozen, staring up at the sky. Never in my life had I seen so much sadness in one place (or so I thought then; now, thinking back, certain mornings of my childhood seem sadder than that lost afternoon of 1973).

The plane came back and flew over us again. It traced a circle over the sea, climbed and returned to Concepción. What a pilot, said Norberto, not even Galland or Rudy Rudler could have done it better, or Hanna Reitsch, or Anton Vogel, or Karl Heinz Schwarz, or Talca's answer to the Wolf of Bremen, or Curicó's Breakneck of Stuttgart, or Hans Marseille himself reincarnate. Then Norberto looked at me and winked. His face was flushed.

In the sky over Concepción the following words appeared: ET VIDIT DEUS . . . LUCEM QUOD . . . ESSET BONA

. . . ET DIVISIT . . . LUCEM AC TENEBRAS. To the east the last letters trailed off among the pencil-shaped clouds proceeding up the Bío-Bío valley. And at one point the plane flew straight up and out of sight, disappearing completely. As if the whole thing were simply a mirage or a nightmare. I heard a miner from Lota ask, What's he written, brother? Half the prisoners at the La Peña Centre, both men and women, were from Lota. No idea, came the reply, but it must be important. Someone else said, Just some crap, but you could hear fear and wonder in the tone of voice. There were more policemen at the entrance to the gymnasium now, six of them whispering amongst themselves. In front of me, Norberto, clasping the fence, scraping and scraping at the ground with his feet as if he were trying to dig a hole, whispered, Either the Blitzkrieg has come again or I'm going totally mad. Calm down, I said. I couldn't be calmer, I'm floating on a cloud, he replied. He took a deep breath and did, in fact, seem to calm down.

Then, preceded by an odd crunching noise, as if someone had stepped on a very large insect or a very small biscuit, the plane reappeared. It was coming in from the sea again. I saw the pointing hands stretch out, the dirty cuffs rise to signal its passage; I heard voices, but perhaps it was only the wind, for in fact, at that moment, no-one dared speak. Norberto squeezed his eyes shut, then opened them very wide. Our Father in heaven, he began, forgive us the sins of our brothers and forgive us our own sins. We are only Chileans, Lord, he went on, innocents, innocents. He said it loud and clear, with a steady voice. Everyone heard him, of course. Some laughed. Behind me I heard anti-clerical wisecracks. I turned around and tried to see who had spoken. Pale and haggard, the faces of the prisoners and policemen were turning like the wheel of fortune. Norberto's face, by contrast, was a still centre. A likeable face, sinking into the earth. Twitching occasionally like the face of a hapless prophet witnessing the arrival of a long-awaited, much-feared Messiah. The plane roared past over our heads. Norberto gripped his elbows as if he were freezing to death.

I caught a glimpse of the pilot. This time he didn't wave. He looked like a stone statue enclosed in the cockpit. The sky was darkening; soon the night would engulf everything. The clouds were no longer pink, but black with streaks of red. Over Concepción the symmetrical outline of the plane looked like a Rorschach blot.

This time it wrote only one word, in larger letters, over what must have been the centre of the city: LEARN. Then, for a moment, it seemed to hesitate and lose altitude, as if it were about to plummet into the roof of a building, as if the pilot had switched off the motor and were giving us a practical demonstration, a first example from which to learn. But only for a moment, the time it took for night and wind to blur the letters of the last word. Then the plane vanished.

For a few seconds no-one said anything. I heard a woman crying on the other side of the fence. Norberto was talking to two young girls, with a very calm expression on his face, as if nothing had happened. It looked as if they were asking him for advice. My God, they were asking a madman for advice! Behind me an unintelligible murmur started up. Something had happened, but in fact it was nothing. Two teachers said something about the church running a publicity campaign. Which church? I asked them. Which church do you think? they said, and turned away. They didn't like me. Then the policemen came out of their daze and made us line up in the yard for a last count. Other voices ordered the women to line up in their yard. Did you enjoy that? asked Norberto. I shrugged. All I know is I'll never forget it, I said. Did you see it was a Messerschmitt? If you say so, I believe you, I said. It was a Messerschmitt, said Norberto, and I think it came from the other world. I slapped him on the back and said, Of course it did. The queue was beginning to move; we were going back into the gymnasium. And it wrote in Latin, said Norberto. Yes, I said, but I didn't understand anything. I did, said Norberto, I wasn't a master typesetter for nothing you know. It was about the beginning of the world, about will, light and darkness. Lux is light. Tenebrae is darkness. Fiat is let there be. Let there be light, get it? Sounds more like an Italian car to me, I said. Well, you're mistaken, brother. And at the end, he wished us all good luck. You think so? I said. Yes, all of us, every one. A poet, I said. Polite, anyway, said Norberto.

3

Carlos Wieder's first poetic performance in the sky over Concepción instantly won him admirers among the nation's enterprising minds.

Soon he was in demand for more sky-writing displays. Initially tentative, the invitations to participate in ceremonies and commemorations were soon being issued with greater frequency and the self-assurance befitting soldiers and gentlemen who know how to recognise a work of art when they see one, whether or not they understand it. Over the airstrip at Las Tencas, for the benefit of a select group of high-ranking officers and businessmen, accompanied by their families (the unmarried daughters were all hopelessly in love with Wieder, while their married sisters were inconsolable), as night was about to fall, he drew a star, the star of our flag, sparkling and solitary over the implacable horizon. A few days later, for a motley and democratic crowd milling among festive marquees at the El Condor air force base, he wrote a poem that an enquiring and well-read spectator described as "*lettriste*". (To be more precise, the opening lines were worthy of Isidore Isou, while the unexpected ending would not have been out of place in a Chilean folk song.) One of the lines alluded obliquely to the Garmendia sisters. They were referred to as "the twins". A hurricane and lips were also mentioned. Although the poem went on to contradict itself, it would have been clear to an informed, attentive reader that the girls were already dead.

In another poem Wieder mentioned a Patricia and a Carmen. "Carmen" was probably the poet Carmen Villagrán, who disappeared at the beginning of December. According to a statement taken by investigators from the Catholic Church, she told her mother she was going to meet a friend and never came back. All her mother had time to ask was, Who's this friend? As she went out of the door, Carmen replied, A poet. Years later, Bibiano O'Ryan identified "Patricia". According to him, it was Patricia Méndez, seventeen years of age, who used to attend a writing workshop run by the Young Communists and who disappeared around the same time as Carmen Villagrán. The differences between the two were striking: Carmen read Michel Leiris in French and came from a middle-class family; Patricia Méndez, as well as being younger, was a working-class girl and a devout follower of Pablo Neruda. She wasn't a university student, like Carmen, although she hoped one day to do teacher training; in the meantime she had a job in an electrical goods shop. Bibiano visited Patricia's mother, who showed him an old school exercise book with poems in it. They were bad, according to Bibiano, under the spell of Neruda at his worst, a mishmash of *Twenty Love Poems* and *Incitation to Nixoncide*, but there was something in them, you could glimpse it, reading between the lines. Freshness, wonder, a taste for life. In any case, wrote Bibiano at the end of his letter, no-one deserves to be killed for writing badly, especially not under the age of twenty.

In his air show at El Condor, Wieder also wrote: *Pupils of Fire*. The generals looking up from the official box assumed, in all sincerity I suppose, that he was writing the names of his sweethearts or his friends, or the professional names of whores from Talcahuano. Some of those who were close to Wieder, however, were aware that he was conjuring up the shades of dead women. But these associates knew nothing about poetry. Or so they thought. (Naturally Wieder disagreed, assuring them they knew more about poetry than most people, more than a good many poets and professors, at any rate, living in their oases or miserably immaculate deserts; but his thugs didn't understand, or dismissed it good-humouredly as another one of the lieutenant's jokes.) For them what Wieder did in his plane was just a "daring feat", daring in more ways than one, but not poetry.

Around the same time, he participated in two other air shows, one in Santiago, where he wrote more verses from the Bible and quotes from *The Rebirth of Chile*, the other in Los Ángeles (in the province of Bío-Bío), where he flew with two other pilots, who unlike him were civilians and had been working as sky-writers for many years. In collaboration, the three of them drew a large (and rather wobbly) Chilean flag in the sky.

Newspaper and radio reports credited Wieder with truly prodigious abilities. No challenge was too great for him. His instructor from the air force academy declared that he was a born pilot: seasoned, instinctive, capable of handling fighter planes and bombers without the slightest difficulty. An old school friend who had once invited Wieder to the family property during the holidays revealed that, to the amazement and subsequent indignation of his parents, the young guest had taken out their dilapidated Piper without permission and landed it on a narrow back road full of potholes. He seems to have spent that summer, presumably the summer of '68, away from his parents (meanwhile, on the other side of the world, the cramped flat of a Parisian caretaker was about to give birth to *Barbaric Writing*, a literary movement that would play a decisive role in the last years of Wieder's life). He was a courageous but shy adolescent (according to his school-friend), given to quite unpredictable outbursts and reckless acts, but in the end he always won the hearts of those who came to know him. My mother and my grandmother adored him (his friend said); they used to say he looked as if he had just come through a storm: vulnerable, drenched to the bone, but with his charm intact.

When it came to the company he kept, however, there were some blots in his copybook: he was known to associate with various shady characters, informers and low-life, with whom he would go out, always at night, to drink or to frequent establishments of ill repute. But all things considered, the blots were just that: accidental blemishes that in no way affected the rest of his character or behaviour, and certainly not his manners. Some even regarded them as indispensable to the career of a writer who aspired to knowledge of the Absolute.

Around that time, the time of the air shows, Wieder's career received a boost from one of Chile's most influential literary critics (although notoriously unreliable as indicators of literary worth, accolades of this kind have carried a great deal of weight in Chile since the time of Alone*), a certain Nicasio Ibacache, who collected antiques and was a devout Catholic, which hadn't prevented him from being a personal friend of Pablo Neruda (and Huidobro before that). He had also corresponded with Gabriela Mistral, been Pablo de Rokha's whipping boy, and (so he said) discovered Nicanor Parra. To cut his c.v. short, he spoke French and English and died in the mid-'80s of a heart attack. In his weekly column in *El Mercurio*, Ibacache published an explication of Wieder's highly individual poetic style. In the article in question he said that we (Chile's literate public) were witnessing the emergence of the new era's major poet. Then, true to form, he went on to give Wieder the benefit of his advice and expatiated in a cryptic and occasionally incoherent fashion on various editions of the Bible, informing us that for his first appearance in the sky over Concepción and the La Peña Centre, Wieder had quoted from the Vulgate, using the edition that includes a Spanish translation by the honourable D. Felipe Scio de S. Miguel, made "in accordance with the interpretations of the Holy Fathers and the Catholic exegetes", published by Gaspar & Roig of Madrid in 1852, as Wieder himself had confided to him one night in the course of a long telephone conversation, during which the critic had asked why the poet

* Pen-name of the critic Hernán Díaz Arrieta (1891–1984)

35

had not used the reverend Fr Scio's translation, to which Wieder had replied, Because Latin makes more of an impression in the sky, although in fact he probably used the word "impact", Latin makes more of an impact in the sky; which didn't prevent him from using Spanish in his subsequent appearances. Naturally Ibacache referred to the various editions of the Bible mentioned by Borges and even to the inauspicious Jerusalem Bible, translated into Spanish by Raimundo Pellegrí and published in Valparaíso in 1875, which, according to the critic, foreshadowed and anticipated the Pacific War that a few years later would bring Chile into conflict with the alliance of Peru and Bolivia. By way of advice, he warned our young poet against the dangers of "premature glory" and the drawbacks of the literary avant-garde, which is prone to "create confusion at the frontiers that separate poetry from painting and theatre or, more precisely, from visual and theatrical events". He stressed the importance of unstinting effort in the task of continuous education; in other words, he encouraged Wieder to keep reading. Read, young man, he seemed to be saying, read the English poets, the French poets, the Chilean poets and Octavio Paz.

Ibacache's tribute, the only article that prolific critic ever devoted explicitly to Wieder, was illustrated with two photographs. The first showed a light aircraft and its pilot in the middle of what appeared to be a minor military airstrip. The photo was taken at a fair distance, so Wieder's features were indistinct. He was wearing a leather jacket with a fur collar, the peaked cap of the Chilean Air Force, jeans and cowboy boots. The caption read: Lieutenant Carlos Wieder on the airstrip at Los Muleros. In the second photo, with a little effort and imagination, one could make out some of the verses that the poet had written in the sky over Los Ángeles as an epilogue to the grand composition of the Chilean flag.

Shortly before the article appeared, I was released from La Peña without charges, as were most of my fellow prisoners there. The first few days back home I didn't go outside at all, which worried my mother and father and provoked ironic comments from my two younger brothers, who were perfectly justified in calling me a coward. After a week, Bibiano O'Ryan came to visit me. When we were alone in my room, he told me he had some good news and some bad news. The good news was that we had been expelled from the university. The bad news was that almost all our friends had disappeared. I said they were probably under arrest or had retreated to their houses in the country, like the Garmendia sisters. No, said Bibiano, the twins have disappeared too. His voice faltered as he said the word "twins". It's hard to explain what happened next (although everything in this story is hard to explain). I was sitting on the end of the bed. Bibiano threw himself into my arms (literally), put his head on my chest and started weeping inconsolably. At first I thought he was having some kind of attack. Then I realised, without the slightest shadow of a doubt, that we would never see the Garmendia sisters again. Bibiano got up, went over to the window and promptly composed himself. It's all speculation, he said with his back to me. Yes, I replied, not knowing what he was referring to. There's a third piece of news, said Bibiano. I might have guessed. Good or bad? I asked.

Frightening, said Bibiano. Go on, I said, before cutting him off, No, wait, let me catch my breath; by which I meant, Let me take a last look at my room, my house, my parents' faces.

That night Bibiano and I went to see Fat Marta. On the surface she seemed the same as ever; or better, more lively. In fact she was hyperactive and couldn't sit still, which made her company irritating after a while. She hadn't been expelled from the university. Life goes on, she said. The main thing was to keep active (any kind of activity would do, like moving a flower-pot five times in half an hour, to stop herself going mad) and to look on the bright side, tackling problems one by one, instead of all at the same time, the way she used to do before. It was a matter of growing up. But we soon discovered what the matter really was: Fat Marta was afraid. She had never been so afraid in her life. I saw Alberto, she said to me. Bibiano nodded. He had already heard the story and I had the impression that certain parts of it struck him as improbable. He rang me, said Marta. He wanted me to go and see him at his flat. I told him he was never home. He asked me how I knew, and laughed. Even then I noticed something odd in his voice, but Alberto has always been kind of secretive so I didn't think any-thing of it. I went to see him. We made a time and I was there on the dot. The house was empty. Wasn't Ruiz-Tagle there? Yes, said Marta, but the flat was empty; there wasn't a single piece of furniture left. Are you moving, Alberto? I asked. Yes, Martita, he said, how did you know? I was very nervous, but I con-trolled myself and said, Everyone's moving these days. He asked me who I meant by "everyone". I told him Diego Soto had left

Concepción. And Carmen Villagrán. And I mentioned you (she meant me), because at the time I didn't know where you'd got to, and the Garmendia sisters. You didn't mention me, asked Bibiano, you didn't say anything about me? No, I didn't say anything about you. And what did Alberto say? Fat Marta looked at me and I realised for the first time that she wasn't just intelligent, but strong as well, and that she was suffering terribly (but not because of the political situation; Marta was suffering because she weighed more than eighty kilos, and she was watching the show, with all its sex and violence, and its love, from a seat in the stalls, cut off from the stage, behind bullet-proof glass). He said, The rats always leave a sinking ship. I couldn't believe my ears. What did you say? I asked. Then Alberto turned and looked at me with a big smile on his face. The game's up, Martita, he said. He was scaring me, so I told him to stop talking in riddles and lighten up. Stop being an arsehole, will you? *Say* something for fuck's sake! I've never been so crude in my life, said Marta. He looked like a snake. No, like a pharaoh. He was just sitting there smiling and watching me, but it was as if he was moving round the empty flat. How could he be moving and sitting still at the same time? The Garmendia sisters are dead, he said. Carmen Villagrán too. I don't believe you, I said. Why would they be dead? You're try-ing to scare me, aren't you, shithead? All the girls who wrote poetry are dead, he said. That's the truth, Martita, you better believe me. We were sitting on the ground. I in one corner and he in the middle of the living room. I was sure he was going to hit me. Any moment, I thought, he's going to jump on me and start beating me up. I came that close to wetting myself. And all this time he's staring at me, staring. I wanted to ask him, What's going to happen to me? But I couldn't. Stop making things up, I whispered. Alberto wasn't listening. It was as if he was waiting for somebody else. For a long time neither of us said anything. At some point, my eyes closed. When I opened them again, he was standing up, leaning against the kitchen door, watching me. You were asleep, Marta, he said to me. Did I snore? I asked him. Yes, he said, you snored. That was when I realised he had a cold. He was holding an enormous yellow handkerchief, which he used to blow his nose twice. You've got the flu, I said, and smiled at him. You'd like that, wouldn't you, Marta? he said. I've just got a bit of a cold. It was a good opportunity to leave, so I stood up and said I'd stop bothering him. You never bother me, he said. You're one of the few women who understand me, Marta, and I appreciate that. But you've caught me on a bad day; I haven't got any wine or whisky or anything. As you can see, I'm in the middle of moving. Of course, I said. I waved good-bye, which is something I don't normally do indoors, and left.

And what happened to the Garmendia sisters? I asked. I don't know, said Fat Marta, emerging from her reverie, how should I know? Why didn't he do anything to you? asked Bibiano. Because we really were friends, I guess, she said.

We went on talking for a long time. *Wieder*, Bibiano informed us, meant "once more", "again", "a second time", and in some contexts "over and over"; or "the next time", in sentences referring to future events. And according to his friend

Anselmo Sanjuán, who had studied German philology at the University of Concepción, it was only in the seventeenth century that the adverb *wieder* and the accusative preposition *wider* came to be spelt differently in order to differentiate their meanings. *Wider* (*widar* or *widari* in Old High German) means "against", "contrary to", and sometimes "in opposition to". And he showered us with examples: *Widerchrist*, "the Antichrist"; *Widerhaken*, "barb, hook"; *widerraten*, "to dissuade"; *Widerlegung*, "refutation, rebuttal"; *Widerlager*, "buttress"; *Widerklage*, "counter-accusation, counter-plea"; *Widernatürlichkeit*, "monstrosity, aberration". For Bibiano each one of these terms was charged with significance. In full flight now, he went on to explain that *Weide* meant "weeping willow", and that *weiden* meant "to graze, to put out to pasture" or "to look after grazing animals", which reminded him of Silva Acevedo's poem "Wolves and Sheep", to which certain readers had attributed a prophetic character. There was more: *weiden* also meant to take morbid pleasure in the contemplation of an object that excites sexual desire and/or sadistic tendencies. At which point Bibiano stared at us, eyes wide open, and we looked back at him, the three of us sitting there quietly, hands clasped, as if in prayer or meditation. And then he returned to Wieder, exhausted and terrified, as if time were not a river but an earthquake happening nearby, and he pointed out that the pilot's grandfather may have been called Weider; perhaps an official at the immigration office, back at the beginning of the century, had made a spelling error and converted his name to Wieder. Unless of course his real name had been *Bieder*, "upright, honest", which was conceivable given the phonetic proximity of the labiodental W and the bilabial B. And finally he remembered that the noun *Widder* meant "ram" or "Aries", from which any number of conclusions could be drawn.

Two days later Fat Marta rang Bibiano and told him that Alberto Ruiz-Tagle was indeed Carlos Wieder. She had recognised him from the photo published in *El Mercurio*. Which was hard to believe, as Bibiano pointed out to me some weeks or months later, since the image was so blurry it could have been almost anyone. What did she have to go on? Her sixth sense, if you ask me, said Bibiano. She says she can recognise Ruiz-Tagle by his posture. In any case, by that time, Ruiz-Tagle had disappeared for good, and Wieder was all we had to give our wretched, empty days some meaning.

Around that time, Bibiano started work as a salesman in a shoe shop. It was a nondescript sort of place, not far from the centre of the city, surrounded by narrow, dimly-lit clothing stores, second-hand bookshops slowly going broke and sad restaurants whose waiters doubled as touts, working the street, making amazing but ambiguously worded offers. Of course we never set foot in a writing workshop again. Occasionally Bibiano would inform me of his projects: he wanted to write stories in English about life in the Irish countryside; he wanted to learn French, at least enough to read Stendhal in the original; he dreamed of barricading himself inside Stendhal and letting the years go by (although he contradicted himself immediately by adding that such a stratagem might work with Chateaubriand, the Octavio Paz of the nineteenth century, but not with

Stendhal, no, definitely not); most of all, he wanted to write a book, an anthology of American Nazi literature. A comprehensive overview, as he used to say when I met him outside the shoe shop at closing time, covering every type of Nazi literature spawned by the Americas, from Canada (the French Canadian writers would be a rich source) to Chile, where he would certainly find variety enough to satisfy all tastes. Meanwhile he had not forgotten Carlos Wieder and was gathering everything he could find about the aviator-poet and his work with the obsessive dedication of a stamp-collector.

One fine day, in 1974 I'm fairly sure it was, the papers informed us that, under the sponsorship of various companies, Carlos Wieder was flying to the South Pole. It was a long and difficult voyage, but at each of his numerous refuelling stops he wrote poems in the sky. These poems, declared his admirers, heralded a new age of iron for the Chilean race. Bibiano followed the journey step by step. Personally, to tell the truth, I no longer cared much what Lieutenant Wieder did or didn't do. At one stage Bibiano showed me a photo, much clearer than the one in which Fat Marta had thought she recognised Ruiz-Tagle. True, there was a resemblance between Ruiz-Tagle and Carlos Wieder, but by that time all I could think about was getting out of the country. In any case, neither the photo nor Wieder's declarations showed even a trace of the old Ruiz-Tagle, so tactful, so considerate and so charmingly shy (after all, he was an autodidact). Wieder was confidence and audacity personified. He spoke of poetry (not Chilean or Latin American poetry, but poetry full stop) with an authority that disarmed all his interviewers (although I should add that, at the time, he was interviewed exclusively by journalists who supported the new regime and would not have dreamt of arguing with an officer of the nation's air force), and although his transcribed replies were full of neologisms and awkward turns of phrase, which are hard to avoid in our intractable language, you could sense a force in the way he talked, the purity and sheen of the absolute, the reflection of a monolithic will.

Before he set off for the Arturo Prat Antarctic base on the last leg of his polar voyage, a gala dinner was held in his honour at a restaurant in Punta Arenas. According to the reports, Wieder drank to excess and slapped a naval officer for having failed to treat a lady with due respect. Concerning this lady the reports vary, but they all coincide on one point: she had not been invited by the organisers and none of the other guests knew her; the only plausible explanations for her presence were that she was a gatecrasher or that she had come with Wieder. He referred to her as "my lady" or "my young lady". She was about twenty-five years old, tall, with dark hair and a shapely figure. At one point in the evening, perhaps during dessert, she shouted at Wieder, You're going to kill yourself tomorrow, Carlos! An appalling lapse of taste, as everyone agreed. That was when the incident with the sailor occurred. Afterwards there were speeches, and the next day, after three or four hours' sleep, Wieder flew to the South Pole. It was, to say the least, an eventful flight, and on more than one occasion the unidentified woman's prediction almost came true (none of the guests ever saw her again, incidentally). When he returned to Punta Arenas,

Wieder declared that the most dangerous thing had been the silence. To the genuine or simulated astonishment of the journalists, he explained that by "silence" he meant the waves of Cape Horn trying to lick the belly of his plane, waves like vast Melvillean whales or severed hands groping at the fuselage throughout the journey, but silently, dumbly, as if in those latitudes sound could only be made by humans. Silence is like leprosy, declared Wieder; silence is like communism; silence is like a blank screen that must be filled. If you fill it, nothing bad can happen to you. If you are pure, nothing bad can happen to you. If you are not afraid, nothing bad can happen to you. According to Bibiano, he was describing an angel. A proudly human angel? I hazarded, quoting Blas de Otero. No, dickhead, replied Bibiano, the angel of our misfortune.

In the crystal clear sky over the Arturo Prat base, Wieder wrote ANTARCTICA IS CHILE, and his exploit was recorded on film and in photographs. He wrote other verses too, about the colour white and the colour black, about ice, the occult and the smile of the Fatherland, a fine, frank, clear-cut smile, a smile *like an eye* that is in fact watching us. Afterwards he returned to Concepción and then went to Santiago, where he appeared on television (I couldn't avoid seeing the programme; there was no TV set in Bibiano's boarding house, so he came round to my place), and yes, Carlos Wieder *was* Ruiz-Tagle (What a nerve, said Bibiano, stealing a good name like that) and yet, in a way, he wasn't, or so it seemed to me. My parents had an old black-and-white TV (they were glad Bibiano was there, watching the programme and having dinner with us, as if they

45

knew I was going to leave and would never have a friend like him again), and Carlos Wieder's photogenic pallor recalled not only the shadowy figure of Ruiz-Tagle, but many other figures, other faces, other phantom pilots who had flown from Chile to Antarctica and back in planes which Mad Norberto, peering from the depths of the night, identified as Messerschmitt fighters, squadrons of Messerchmitts that had escaped from the Second World War. But Wieder, we knew, did not fly in a squadron. He flew a light plane and he flew alone.

4

L ike the story of Chile itself in those years, the story of
Juan Stein, who ran our poetry workshop, is larger than
life.

Born in 1945, he published two books before the coup, one in
Concepción (with a print run of five hundred) and another in
Santiago (five hundred copies again). Together, they came to less
than fifty pages. His poems were short. Like most of the poets of
his generation, he was influenced by Nicanor Parra and Ernesto
Cardenal, but also by Jorge Teillier's home-grown imagism,
although Stein recommended we read Lihn rather than Teillier.
His tastes were quite often different from and even opposed to
our own: he didn't care for Jorge Cáceres (the Chilean surrealist
who had become our cult hero) or Rosamel del Valle or Anguita.
He liked Pezoa Véliz (and knew some of his poems by heart),
Magallanes Moure (a foible for which we compensated by dipping
into the verse of the dreadful Braulio Arenas), the geographical
and gastronomical poems of Pablo de Rokha (which we, and
when I say we, I realise now I am referring only to Bibiano O'Ryan
and myself; as to the others, I can't remember a thing about

them, not even their literary loves and hates; in any case we kept well clear of de Rokha, as if he were a bottomless pit, and anyway you're better off reading Rabelais), Neruda's love poetry and *Residence on Earth* (which we, having suffered from Neruditis since early childhood, could not so much as look at without coming out in hives). We shared Stein's esteem for the aforementioned Parra, Lihn and Teillier, although we differed over the relative merits of certain works (the publication of *Artefacts*, which we adored, prompted Stein to write a letter to old Nicanor, in a tone somewhere between indignation and perplexity, reproaching him for some of the jokes he had seen fit to crack at that crucial moment in Latin America's revolutionary struggle. Parra replied on the back of an *Artefacts* postcard, telling him not to worry, because no-one, on the right or the left, was reading anyway, and I'm sure Stein treasured that card). We also liked Armando Uribe Arce, Gonzalo Rojas and some of the poets from Stein's generation, born in the '40s, whom we used to frequent, mainly because they happened to live in the area; we had no particular aesthetic affinities with them, but in the end they probably influenced us more than anyone else. Juan Luis Martínez (who, for us, was a compass lost in the wilds of Chile), Oscar Hahn (who was born at the end of the '30s, but that didn't matter), Gonzalo Millán (who came to the workshop twice and read his poems, which were all short, but there were *lots* of them), Claudio Bertoni (who was almost young enough to qualify as one of our generation: the poets born in the '50s), Jaime Quezada (who got drunk with us one day, knelt down and started bellowing a novena),

Waldo Rojas (who was one of the first to distance himself from the so-called "accessible poetry" that was all the rage at the time – cut-price versions of Parra and Cardenal) and, of course, Diego Soto, who according to Stein, was the best poet of his generation, and according to us was one of the *two* best, the other being Stein himself.

We would often go to his house, Bibiano and I, a little house near the station that Stein, who was a lecturer at the University of Concepción, had been renting since his student days. There were maps everywhere, more maps than books it seemed. That was the first thing that struck Bibiano and me; we were surprised to see so few books (Diego Soto's house, by contrast, was like a library). Maps of Chile, Argentina and Peru, maps of the Andes, a road map of Central America that I have never seen anywhere else, published by a Protestant church in North America, maps of Mexico, maps showing the conquest of Mexico and the advance of the Mexican Revolution, maps of France, Spain, Germany and Italy, a map of the English railway system and a map showing train journeys in English literature, maps of Greece and Egypt, Israel and the Middle East, Jerusalem in ancient and modern times, India and Pakistan, Burma and Cambodia, a map of the mountains and rivers of China and one of the Shinto temples of Japan, a map of the Australian desert and one of Micronesia, a map of Easter Island and a map of the town of Puerto Montt in southern Chile.

Juan Stein possessed a great many maps, as people often do when they have a passionate but unrequited desire to travel.

There were also two framed photographs hanging on the

wall. Both were in black and white. In one, you could see a man and a woman sitting by the doorway of their house. The man looked like Juan Stein, with straw-coloured hair and very deep-set blue eyes. It was a photo of his mother and father, he told us. The other one was a portrait – an official portrait – of a Red Army general called Ivan Chernyakhovsky. According to Stein, he was the greatest general of the Second World War. Bibiano, who knew about these things, mentioned Zhukov, Koniev, Rokossovsky, Vatutin and Malinovsky, but Stein stood firm: Zhukov was brilliant and cold, Koniev was a hard man, Rokossovsky had talent and the help of Zhukov, Vatutin was a good general but no better than the German generals he was pitted against, you could say the same of Malinovsky really, none of them was a patch on Chernyakhovsky (to equal him you'd have to roll Zhukov, Vasilevsky and the three best tank commanders into one). Chernyakhovsky had innate talent (if there is such a thing in the art of war), he was loved by his men (in so far as the rank and file can love a general) and he was young, the youngest general in charge of an army (known as a front in the Soviet Union), and one of the few high-ranking officers to die in the front line, in 1945, when the war was already won, at the age of thirty-nine.

We soon realized that there was something more between Stein and Chernyakhovsky than an admiration for the strategic and tactical gifts of the Soviet general. One afternoon, during a conversation about politics, we asked him how he, a Trotskyist, could have lowered himself to ask the Soviet Embassy for the general's photo. We were joking, but Stein took us seriously, confessing that the photo had been a gift from his mother, who was Ivan Chernyakhovsky's cousin. She was the one who had requested the photo from the Embassy, many years back, as a blood relative of the hero. When Stein had left home to come and study in Concepción, his mother had given him the photo without a word of explanation. He went on to tell us about the Chernyakhovskys, a family of dirt-poor Ukrainian Jews, and the various destinies that had scattered them all over the world. It turned out that his mother's father was the brother of the general's father, which made him one of the great man's third cousins. Our admiration for Stein was already unconditional, but after that revelation it knew no bounds. Over the years we learnt more about Chernyakhovsky: he commanded an armoured division in the first months of the war, the 28th Tank Division, which was driven back through the Baltic Republics to the vicinity of Novgorod. Then he was at a loose end until he was given the command of a corps (which in Soviet military terminology is equivalent to a division) in the region of Voronezh; this corps was part of the 60th Army, and when, during the Nazi offensive in '42, the commander of the Army was dismissed, his post was offered to Chernyakhovsky, the youngest of the eligible officers, which naturally provoked jealousy and suspicion among his comrades. We learnt that, in this new post, he served under Vatutin (who was then commanding the Voronezh Front, which in Russian military terminology is equivalent to an army, but I think I already said that), whom he respected and admired; that he converted the 60th Army into an invincible fighting machine, steadily advancing through

Russia and then through the Ukraine; nothing and no-one could stop it. In 1944 he was promoted to the command of a front, the Third Belorussian Front, and during the '44 offensive he played a key role in destroying the Army Group Centre, consisting of four German armies, and this was probably the greatest blow suffered by the Nazis in the Second World War, worse than the siege of Stalingrad or the Normandy landings, worse than Operation Cobra and the crossing of the Dnepr (in which Chernyakhovsky took part), worse than the counter-offensive in the Ardennes or the battle of Kursk (in which he also took part). We discovered that of the Russian armies which participated in Operation Bagration (the destruction of the Army Group Centre), by far the most distinguished was the Third Belorussian Front, which advanced unstoppably, with unprecedented speed and penetration, and was the first to arrive in Eastern Prussia. We also found out that Chernyakhovsky had lost his parents when he was an adolescent, and had boarded in other people's houses, with other people's families, that he was mocked and humiliated for being a Jew, but proved to those who insulted him that he was not only their equal but their superior, that as a child he had witnessed the followers of the Ukrainian nationalist Petliura torturing then trying to assassinate his father in the village of Verbovo (with its little white houses scattered over the slopes of the rolling hills), that his adolescence was a mixture of Dickens and Makarenko, that during the war he lost his brother Alexander, which intelligence was kept from him for an afternoon and a whole night because he was in the midst of an offensive, that he died alone in the middle of a road, that he was twice named Hero of the Soviet Union, awarded the Order of Lenin, four Orders of the Red Banner, two Orders of Suvorov (first class), the Order of Kutuzov (first class), the order of Bogdan Jmelnitzki (first class), and numerous, countless medals, that by order of the Government and the Party monuments to him were erected in Vilnius and Vinnitsa (no doubt the one in Vilnius has disappeared and the one in Vinnitsa has probably been torn down too), that the city of Insterburg in the old Eastern Prussia is now called Chernyakhovsk in his honour, that the kolkhoz for the village of Verbovo in the district of Tomashpol is also named after him (although the kolkhoz is a thing of the past), and that in the village of Oksino in the district of Umanski in the region of Cherkassy, a bronze bust was set up to commemorate the great general (I'd bet a month's pay the bust has been replaced; Petliura's the hero now and tomorrow, who knows?). To sum up, as Bibiano said, quoting Parra: that's how it goes, the glory of the world; no glory, no world, not even a miserable mortadella sandwich.

In any case, on the wall of Juan Stein's house, there hung a rather ornately framed portrait of Chernyakhovsky, and that, I dare say, was incommensurably more important than the busts and the cities named after him and the countless Chernyakhovsky Streets, full of potholes, scattered through the Ukraine, Belorussia, Lithuania and Russia. I don't know why I've kept the photo, Stein said to us. Maybe because he was the only really important Jewish general in the Second World War and he came to a tragic end. Though the real reason is probably that my mother gave it to me when I left home, like a sort of riddle. She didn't say a word, just handed me the picture. Was she trying to tell me something? Was it meant to be the start of a dialogue? Et cetera, et cetera. The Garmendia sisters thought the photo of Chernyakhovsky was awful. They would have liked to replace it with a portrait of Blok (*there* was a good-looking Russian) or Mayakovsky, their dream lover. Sometimes, especially when he was drunk, Stein would wonder what Ivan Chernyakhovsky's third cousin was doing in the literature department of a university in southern Chile. And sometimes he said he was going to use the frame for a photo he had of William Carlos Williams doing his day-job as a small-town doctor. In the photo he was carrying a black leather bag and there was a stethoscope, like a two-headed snake, emerging, in fact almost falling, from the pocket of his old jacket, which was showing its years, but comfortable and still warm in the cold weather, and the footpath he was walking down was long and tranquil, edged with picket fences painted white or green or red, behind which you could glimpse little patios or strips of lawn (and a mower left out by someone who had been called away, perhaps). Dr Williams was wearing a dark, narrow-brimmed hat, and perfectly clean, almost sparkling glasses, yet there was nothing extreme or excessive about their brightness; he didn't look intensely happy or sad, but content (perhaps because he was warmly wrapped up in his jacket, perhaps because he knew that the patient he was going to see was not fatally ill), walking along calmly, at, say, five o'clock on a winter's evening.

But Stein never replaced the portrait of Chernyakhovsky with his photo of William Carlos Williams. Some of us in the workshop, and Stein himself on occasion, had doubts about the authenticity of the photo. According to the Garmendia sisters, it looked more like President Truman disguised as *something*, not necessarily a doctor, walking down the street in his home town, incognito. In Bibiano's view, it was a clever montage: Williams's face with someone else's body, some other small-town doctor probably, while the background was a mosaic: the wooden fences taken from one picture, the lawn and the lawn-mower from another; then there were the birds perched on the fences and even on the mower-handle, the light-grey evening sky; in all eight or nine different photos had been used. Stein was baffled, but he wasn't ruling out any possibilities. Whatever its origins, he used to call it "the photo of Dr Williams" and he didn't throw it out (sometimes he called it "the photo of Dr Norman Rockwell" or "the photo of Dr William Rockwell"). It was clearly one of his most treasured possessions, not that, poor as he was, he had many to treasure. On one occasion (I think we were discussing beauty and truth) Veronica Garmendia asked him why he was so attached to the photo when it almost certainly wasn't Williams. I just like it, said Stein. I like to think it *is* William Carlos Williams. But most of all, he added after a while, by which stage we had already got onto Gramsci, I like its tranquillity, the idea that Williams is going about his business, walking unhurriedly down a calm street to make a house call. And later still, when we were talking about poetry and the Paris Commune, he said very softly, I don't know; but I don't think anyone heard.

After the coup, Stein disappeared, and for a long time Bibiano and I assumed he was dead.

In fact everyone assumed he was dead; everyone thought they were bound to have killed that Jewish Bolshevik son of a bitch. One afternoon Bibiano and I went to his house. We were afraid to knock at the door. In our paranoia we imagined that the house might be under surveillance; we even thought a policeman might open the door, invite us in and never let us out again. So we walked past the house three or four times. There were no lights on, and we went away feeling deeply ashamed but also secretly relieved. A week later, by tacit accord, we returned to Stein's house. No-one answered our knock. A woman watched us from the window of the adjoining house, then disappeared, and as well as reviving a host of vague cinematic memories, this heightened the effect that Stein's house and the whole street had on us, making us feel even more alone and deserted. The third time we went there, a young woman opened the door, followed by two children, both under three, one walking, the other on all fours. She told us she was living there now with her husband and hadn't met the previous tenant. She said that if we wanted to find out more we'd have to go and talk to the landlady. She was a kind woman. She invited us in and offered us a cup of tea, which Bibiano and I declined. We don't want to bother you, we said. The maps and the photo of General Chernyakhovsky were gone from the walls. This man was a good friend of yours and he left suddenly, without telling you? asked the woman, smiling. Yes, we said, something like that.

Shortly afterwards I left Chile for good.

Some time later – I can't remember if I was living in Mexico or in France – I received a very short letter from Bibiano, so telegraphic in style it was almost a riddle or a piece of nonsense (but one thing was clear, at least: he was happy), accompanied by a press cutting, probably from a Santiago newspaper. The article mentioned various "Chilean terrorists" who had crossed into Nicaragua from Costa Rica with the Sandinista troops. One of them was Juan Stein.

From then on there was no shortage of news about Stein. He appeared and disappeared like a ghost wherever there was fighting, wherever desperate, generous, mad, courageous, despicable Latin Americans were destroying, rebuilding and redestroying reality, in a final bid that was doomed to failure. I saw him in a documentary about the capture of Rivas, a town in southern Nicaragua, with a ragged haircut, thinner than before, dressed like a cross between a soldier and a professor at a summer school, smoking a pipe, his broken glasses held together with wire. Bibiano sent me a cutting in which it was reported that Stein, along with five other ex-members of the MIR, was fighting the South Africans in Angola. Later I received two photocopied pages from a Mexican magazine (so by then I must have been in Paris) which referred to conflicts between the Cubans in Angola and certain international groups, one of which consisted of two Chilean adventurers, the sole survivors (or so they said, and I presume the journalist interviewed them in a bar in Luanda, from which I deduce that they were drunk), supposedly the sole survivors of a group known as the Flying Chileans, which reminded me of the Human Eagles, a circus that used to do marathon tours of southern Chile every year. Stein, of course, was one of these survivors. From Angola, it seems, he went to Nicaragua. In Nicaragua we kept losing track of him. He was lieutenant to a priest and guerrilla leader who died in the capture of Rivas. Then he commanded a battalion or a brigade or was second in charge of something or withdrew from the front line to train new recruits. He didn't take part in the triumphal entry into Managua. Then he disappeared again for some time. He was rumoured to be among the members of the commando that assassinated Somoza in Paraguay. He was rumoured to have joined a Colombian guerrilla group. Some even said he had returned to Africa, and was in Angola or Mozambique or with the Namibian guerrilla fighters. He lived dangerously, but as they say in the westerns, the bullet with his name on it was still waiting to be cast. Then he went back to America and for a while he lived in Managua. Bibiano told me that an Argentine poet called Di Angeli, one of his correspondents, had been involved in organising a reading of poetry from Argentina, Uruguay and Chile at the Managua Cultural Centre, during which a member of the audience, "a tall, fair-haired guy with glasses", made various remarks about Chilean poetry and the criteria used to select the poems for the reading (the organisers, including Di Angeli, had prohibited the inclusion of poems by Nicanor Parra and Enrique Lihn for political reasons); in a word, he said it was a load of shit, at least the Chilean section, but the way he said it was very calm, not at all aggressive, according to Di Angeli, very ironic and a bit sad or tired, maybe, hard to tell. (Of the countless correspondents scattered throughout the world with whom Bibiano maintained regular epistolary contact from his shoe shop in Concepción, this Di Angeli was, by the way, one of the most shameless, cynical and amusing. Although a typical leftist social climber, he was constantly apologising for oversights and errors of all kinds; his gaffes, according to Bibiano, were legendary. Under Stalin, his pathetic existence could have inspired a great picaresque novel, but in Latin America in the '70s, it was just a pathetic existence, full of little acts of meanness, some of which were not even intentional. He would have been better off on the right, said Bibiano, but, curiously, among the hosts of the left, Di Angeli's kind are legion. At least he hasn't started writing literary criticism, remarked Bibiano, adding that it wouldn't be long. And sure enough, one day in the abominable '80s, looking through some Mexican and Argentine magazines, I came across various critical articles by Di Angeli. I think he had made a name for himself. I haven't encountered his by-line again in the '90s, but I don't read as many magazines these days.) Stein, in any case, was back in America. And it was definitely the Juan Stein we knew from Concepción, according to Bibiano, the third cousin of Ivan Chernyakhovksy. For some time, the time of an overly drawn-out sigh, he was to be seen at gatherings such as the aforementioned reading of South American poetry or at exhibitions or in the company of Ernesto Cardenal (twice) or at the theatre. Then he disappeared and was never seen again in Nicaragua. He hadn't gone very far. Some said he was with the Guatemalan guerrilla fighters; others swore that he had joined the Frente

Farabundo Martí (FMLN). Bibiano and I agreed that a guerrilla group with a name like that deserved to have Stein on its side. Although, given the chance, we felt he would have personally executed those responsible for the death of Roque Dalton (viewed from a distance, Stein cut a fierce and implacable figure; he had taken on the epic proportions of a Hollywood hero). How could one dream, or one nightmare, possibly accommodate the third cousin of Chernyakhovsky, the Jewish Bolshevik from the forests of southern Chile, and the sons of bitches who killed Roque Dalton while he was *asleep*, just to shut him up, for their revolutionary convenience? It was inconceivable. Yet Stein was there in El Salvador. And he participated in various campaigns and surprise attacks and one fine day he disappeared and this time it was for good. I was living in Spain at that stage, doing various menial jobs; I didn't have a television and rarely bought a newspaper. According to Bibiano, Juan Stein was killed in the FMLN's widely reported final offensive, during which they succeeded in taking control of certain sectors of San Salvador. I remember seeing snatches of that distant war while eating or drinking in bars in Barcelona, but although people were watching the television, the noise of the conversations and the plates and cutlery being carried back and forth made it impossible to hear anything. Even the images my memory has retained (from the war correspondents' video tapes) are blurred and fragmentary. There are only two things I remember with absolute clarity: the pitiful barricades in the streets of San Salvador, more like fairground shooting stands, and the small, dark, wiry figure of an FMLN commander. He was known as Commander Achilles or Commander Ulysses and I know that shortly after speaking to the journalist he was killed. According to Bibiano, all the commanders involved in that desperate offensive had assumed the names of Greek heroes and demigods. What could Stein's name have been? Commander Patroclus? Commander Hector? Commander Paris? I don't know. But certainly not Aeneas. Or Ulysses. When the battle was over and the bodies were being removed, among them was the corpse of a tall, fair-haired man. A brief description in the police records indicated that there were scars from old wounds on the arms and legs, and a lion rampant tattooed on the right arm. It was a high quality tattoo. A real professional job, honest to God, you couldn't get that done in El Salvador. In the file at Central Police Records the mysterious fair-haired man was identified as Jacobo Sabotinski, an Argentine citizen and ex-member of the Ejército Revolucionario del Pueblo (ERP).

Many years later, Bibiano went to Puerto Montt to look for Juan Stein's family home. He couldn't find anyone called Stein. There was a Stone, two Steiners and three Steens. The Stone he eliminated straight away. The Steens were all related and they couldn't tell him much; they weren't Jewish and they didn't know anything about the Stein family or Chernyakhovsky. They asked Bibiano if he was Jewish himself and if there was money in it. By this stage, I think, Puerto Montt had started to boom. The Steiners were Jewish, but came from Poland, not the Ukraine. The first one he went to see was a tall, overweight agronomist, who wasn't much help. Then he talked with the agronomist's aunt, a high school piano teacher. She remembered a widow called Stein who had gone to live in Llanquihue in 1974. But she wasn't Jewish, that lady, declared the piano teacher. Slightly confused, Bibiano went to Llanquihue. What she must have meant, he thought, was that the widow wasn't a *practising* Jew. In any case, knowing Juan Stein and his family history (his third cousin having been a Red Army general), he would have expected them to be atheists.

It didn't take him long to find old Mrs Stein's house in Llanquihue. It was a little wooden house painted green, on the outskirts of the village. When he went in through the gate, a friendly dog, white with black splotches like a miniature cow, came out to greet him. He rang the doorbell, which sounded like – and may well have been – a real bell with a clapper, and after a while a woman opened the door. She must have been about thirty-five and was one of the most beautiful women Bibiano had ever seen.

He asked if Mrs Stein lived there. She used to, but a long time ago, replied the woman cheerfully. What a pity, said Bibiano. I've been trying to find her for ten days now and I'll have to go back to Concepción soon. The woman invited him in, told him she was about to have morning tea and asked if he would like to join her. Bibiano, of course, said yes, and then the woman confessed that old Mrs Stein had been dead for three years. A sudden wave of sadness seemed to sweep over her and Bibiano felt he was to blame. She had known Mrs Stein and, although she wouldn't have said they were friends, she respected her: a slightly domineering woman, one of those stern

62

Germans, but she had a good heart. I didn't know her, said Bibiano. In fact, I was trying to find her to pass on the news of her son's death, but perhaps it's better this way; it's always terrible having to tell someone that one of their children has died. There must be some mistake, said the woman. She only had one son, who was still living when she died, and he *was* a friend of mine. Bibiano thought he was going to choke on his avocado sandwich. Only one son? Yes, a bachelor, very nice looking, I don't know why he never got married. I guess because he was so shy. Then I must have got mixed up again, said Bibiano. We must be talking about different families. So Mrs Stein's son doesn't live in Llanquihue any more? He died last year in a hospital in Valdivia, so I heard. We were friends, but I never went to see him in hospital, we weren't that close. What did he die of? I think it was cancer, said the woman, looking at Bibiano's hands. And he was left-wing wasn't he? asked Bibiano, with a faltering voice. Could have been, said the woman, suddenly cheerful again – her eyes shone like no other eyes I've ever seen, said Bibiano – yes, he was left-wing, but he wasn't militant; he was one of the silent left, like so many Chileans since 1973. He wasn't Jewish, was he? No, said the woman, although who knows, I've never really been interested in religion, but no, I don't think they were Jewish, they were German. What was his name? Juan Stein. Juanito Stein. And what did he do? He was a teacher, although what he really liked was repairing motors: tractors, harvesters, pumps, any kind of motor, he had a real gift for it. And he made a nice bit of pocket money that way. Sometimes he made the parts himself. Juanito

Stein. Is he buried in Valdivia? I think so, said the woman, looking sad again.

So Bibiano went to the cemetery in Valdivia and, with the help of one of the attendants to whom he promised a handsome tip, spent a whole day looking for the grave of that tall, fair-haired Juan Stein who never left Chile, but despite his efforts he couldn't find it.

5

A   t the end of 1973 or the beginning of 1974, Diego Soto, Juan Stein's best friend and rival, also disappeared. They were always together (except at their respective workshops) and always talking about poetry. If the sky over Chile had begun to crumble and fall, they would have gone on talking about poetry: the tall, fair-haired Stein and the short, dark Soto; one strong and well built, the other's fine-boned body hinting at future plumpness. Stein was mainly interested in Latin American poetry, while Soto was translating French poets unknown in Chile at the time (many of them, I fear, still are), and this, of course, infuriated a lot of people. How could that ugly little Indian presume to translate and correspond with Alain Jouffroy, Denis Roche and Marcelin Pleynet? Michel Bulteau, Mathieu Messagier, Claude Pelieu, Franck Venaille, Pierre Tilman, Daniel Biga . . . who *were* these people, for God's sake? And what was so special about this Georges Perec character, published by Denoël, whose books Soto was always toting around, pretentious bastard. When he was no longer to be seen walking the streets of Concepción with books under his arm, always neatly dressed (as opposed to Stein, who looked like a tramp), heading off to the Faculty of Medicine or standing in a queue outside some cinema or theatre, when he disappeared into thin air, nobody missed him. Many would have been glad to hear of his death, for reasons that were not so much political (Soto was a socialist sympathiser, but that was all, he wasn't even a faithful socialist voter; I would have described him as a left-wing pessimist) as aesthetic in nature: the pleasure of knowing you're finally rid of someone who is more intelligent than you are and more knowledgeable and who lacks the social grace to hide it. Writing this now it seems hard to believe. But that's how it was. Soto's enemies would have been able to forgive his biting wit, but they could never forgive his indifference. His indifference and his intelligence.

Soto, however, like Stein (whom he no doubt never saw again), reappeared in exile. First he went to East Germany, but left as soon as he could after several unpleasant experiences. According to the melancholy folklore of exile – made up of stories that, as often as not, are fabrications or pale copies of what really happened – one night another Chilean gave him such a terrible beating that he ended up in a Berlin hospital with head injuries and two broken ribs. He moved to France where he scraped a living teaching Spanish and English, and translating for small presses, mainly books by eccentric, early twentieth-century Latin American writers with a bent for fantasy or pornography, or both, as in the case of Pedro Pereda, an obscure novelist from Valparaiso, the author of a startling story in which a woman finds vaginas and anuses growing, or rather opening, all over her anatomy, to the understandable horror of her friends and family (the story is set in the '20s, but I don't suppose it would have been any less shocking in the '70s or the '90s), and who ends up confined to a brothel for miners in northern Chile, where she remains, shut up in a room without windows, until in the end she becomes a great amorphous, uncontrollable "in-and-out", finishes off the old pimp who runs the brothel along with the rest of the whores and the terrified clients, goes out onto the patio and sets off into the desert (walking or flying, Pereda doesn't say), finally disappearing into thin air.

Soto also tried (unsuccessfully) to translate Sophie Podolski, the Belgian poet who committed suicide at the age of twenty-one, and Pierre Guyotat, the author of *Eden, Eden, Eden* and *Prostitution* (again he gave up), and *La Disparition* by Georges Perec, a detective story written without using the letter *e*, which he managed (with a limited degree of success) to render into Spanish, following in the footsteps of Jardiel Poncela, who, half a century earlier, had written a story in which the aforementioned vowel was conspicuous by its absence. But it is one thing to *write* without using *e* and quite another to *translate* without it.

For a while, Soto and I were both living in Paris, but I never saw him. At the time I had no desire to look up old friends. Also, from what I'd been told, Soto's financial situation had improved; he had married a French woman. Later I heard that they had a child (for what it's worth, by then I was living in Spain). He regularly attended the meetings of Chilean writers held in Amsterdam, and contributed to poetry magazines in Mexico, Argentina and Chile. I think he even had a book published in Buenos Aires or Madrid. Then I heard from a friend that Soto was lecturing at a university, which meant financial stability and time for writing and research, and by that stage he had two children, a boy and a girl. He had no plans to return to Chile. He must have been happy, reasonably happy. I could imagine his comfortable flat in Paris, or a house perhaps, in a village not far from the city. I could see him reading in the silence of his soundproof study, while the children watched television and his wife cooked or ironed, because, well, someone has to do the cooking, but of course it could have been a maid, yes, a Portuguese or an African maid, so Soto could read in his soundproof study, or write perhaps, although he was never very prolific, without feeling guilty, while his wife was busy in her own study, near the children's room, or sitting at a nineteenth-century desk in a corner of the living room, correcting exam papers or planning a summer holiday or idly casting an eye over the cinema listings to decide which film they would go and see that night.

According to Bibiano (who exchanged letters with him quite regularly), it wasn't so much that Soto had become middle-class: he had never been anything else. If books and reading are what count, you have to lead a sedentary, middle-class life to some degree, said Bibiano. Take me, for example: working in the shoe shop – which gets more depressing every year, or more amusing, I can't really tell – living in the same old boarding house . . . in a way, on a different scale, I'm doing the same thing as Soto (or letting the same thing happen to me).

In a word, Soto was happy. He thought he had escaped the curse (or we thought he had, anyway; Soto, I suspect, never believed in curses).

Then he received an invitation to participate in a conference on literature and criticism in Latin America, to be held in Alicante.

It was winter. Soto hated flying; he had done it only once in his life, at the end of 1973, when he flew from Santiago to Berlin. So after a whole night in the train he stepped off in Alicante. It was a weekend conference, but instead of going back to Paris on Sunday night, Soto stayed on. It is not known why. On Monday morning he bought a ticket for Perpignan. The trip was uneventful. When he arrived at the station in Perpignan he enquired about departures for Paris that night and bought a ticket for the 1.00 a.m. train. He spent the rest of the afternoon walking around the city, stopping in bars. He visited a second-hand bookshop where he bought a book by Guerau de Carrera, an avant-garde Franco-Catalan poet who died during the Second World War, but to pass the time he read a detective novel he had picked up that morning in Alicante (Vásquez Montalbán? Juan Madrid?) but didn't have time to finish (the folded corner of page 155 seemed to indicate that he read no further) despite having devoured the first part with the voracity of an adolescent during the train journey.

In Perpignan he ate in a pizzeria. It is odd that he didn't go to a good restaurant to sample the renowned cuisine of Rousillon, but for whatever reason he went to a pizzeria. The coroner's report is explicit and leaves not a shadow of doubt. Soto had a green salad, a large plate of canneloni, an enormous (and I mean *truly* enormous) helping of chocolate, strawberry, vanilla and banana ice cream, and two cups of black coffee. He also consumed a bottle of Italian red wine (perhaps not the best choice to go with the canneloni, but I know nothing about wine). During the meal he read both the detective novel and *Le Monde*, jumping back and forth. He left the pizzeria at about 10.00 p.m.

According to various witnesses, he arrived at the station around midnight. He had an hour to kill before the departure of his train. He went to the station bar and ordered a coffee. He was carrying his bag, and, in the other hand, the book by Carrera, the detective novel and the copy of *Le Monde*. According to the waiter who served him, he was sober.

He didn't spend more than ten minutes in the bar. A railway employee saw him walking up and down the platforms, slowly but steadily. Certainly not drunk. Presumably he disappeared among the station's labyrinthine paths, dear to Salvador Dalí. No doubt that is precisely what he wanted to do. To lose himself for an hour in the sovereign magnificence of Perpignan railway station. To retrace the mathematical, astronomical or mythical itinerary that, in Dalí's dream, was hidden for all to see within the confines of that edifice. To be a tourist, in other words. The tourist Soto had always been since he left Concepción. A Latin American tourist, perplexed and desperate in equal parts (Gómez Carrillo is our Virgil), but a tourist nevertheless.

What happened next is uncertain. Soto lost himself in the cathedral or cosmic transmitter that is the Perpignan railway station. Because of the time and the weather (it was winter), the station was almost empty despite the fact that the 1.00 a.m. train for Paris was about to leave. Most people were in the bar or the main waiting room. Soto, for some reason, perhaps he heard voices, went to look in another room, some way off. There he found three young neo-Nazis and a bundle on the ground. The youths were diligently kicking the bundle. Soto froze on the threshold until he realised that the bundle was moving, when he saw first a hand and then an incredibly dirty arm emerging from the rags. The tramp shouted, Stop hitting me. It was a woman's voice. But no-one was listening, no-one except the Chilean writer. Perhaps his eyes filled with tears, tears of self-pity, because something told him he had met his destiny. Now he wouldn't have to choose between Tel Quel and the OuLiPo. For him, life had chosen the crime reports. In any case, he dropped his bag and the books at the door and approached the youths. Before the fight began he insulted them in Spanish. The harsh Spanish of southern Chile. The youths stabbed Soto and ran away.

There was a brief article in the Catalonian newspapers, but Bibiano told me all about it, in a very detailed letter, almost like a detective's report. It was the last letter I received from him.

At first I was annoyed that he had stopped writing to me, but then, considering the fact that I hardly ever replied, I realised it was understandable and didn't hold it against him. Years later

I heard a story that I would have liked to tell Bibiano, but by then I wasn't sure of his address. It was the story of Petra, and, in a way, Petra is to Soto what Juan Stein's double is to the Juan Stein we knew. Petra's story should be told like a fairy tale: Once upon a time in Chile there was a poor little boy . . . I think the boy was called Lorenzo, I'm not sure, and I've forgotten his surname, but some readers may remember it, and he liked to play, and climb trees and high-tension pylons. One day he climbed up a pylon and got such a shock that he lost both his arms. They had to amputate them just below the shoulders. So Lorenzo grew up in Chile without arms, an unfortunate situation for any child, but he also grew up in Pinochet's Chile, which turned unfortunate situations into desperate ones, on top of which he soon discovered that he was homosexual, which made his already desperate situation inconceivable and indescribable.

Given these circumstances, it is not surprising that Lorenzo became an artist. (What else could he do?) But it's hard to be an artist in the third world if you are poor, have no arms and are gay to boot. So, for a time, Lorenzo had to do other things. He studied and improved himself. He sang in the streets. Being a hopeless romantic, he fell in love. His disappointments (not to mention humiliations, put-downs and insults) were terrible, and one day – to be marked retrospectively with a white stone – he decided to kill himself. One particularly sad summer evening, as the sun sank into the Pacific Ocean, Lorenzo jumped into the sea from a rock used exclusively by suicides (every self-respecting stretch of Chilean coastline has one). He sank like a stone with his eyes open and saw the water grow darker and the bubbles streaming from his lips and then an involuntary movement of his legs sent him back up to the surface. Because of the waves he couldn't see the beach, only the rocks and the masts of pleasure craft or fishing boats. Then he went under again. This time too he kept his eyes open: he turned his head calmly (as if under anaesthetic), looking for something, anything, as long as it was beautiful, to be his last memory. But darkness enveloped whatever else might have been sinking with him into the depths and he could see nothing. Then, as the saying goes, his whole life flashed before him like a film. Some parts were in black and white, others in colour. His poor mother's love, her pride, her weariness, how she hugged him at night when, in Chile's poor neighbourhoods everything seemed to be hanging by a thread (black and white); the trembling, the nights when he wet his bed, the hospitals, the staring, the zoo-like staring (colour); friends sharing what little they had, the consolations of music, marijuana, beauty revealed in unlikely places (black and white); love perfect and brief like a sonnet by Góngora; knowing with a fatal certainty (but raging against the knowledge) that you only live once. Suddenly drawing courage from nowhere, he decided he was not going to die. Now or never, he thought, and began to swim back up. It seemed to take forever to reach the surface and then he could hardly bear to keep himself afloat, but he did. That afternoon he learnt to swim without arms, like an eel or a snake. In the current socio-political climate, he said to himself, committing suicide is absurd and redundant. Better to become an undercover poet.

From that day on he began to paint (with his mouth and

his feet), he took up dancing, he started writing poems and love letters, he learnt to play musical instruments and compose songs (a photo shows him playing the piano with his toes, smiling at the camera), and he began to save money so that he could get out of Chile.

It was hard, but he managed to leave in the end. In Europe, of course, life wasn't much easier. For some time, years perhaps (though Lorenzo, who was younger than Bibiano and me, and much younger than Soto and Stein, left Chile when the flood of emigrants had abated), he made a living as a street musician and dancer in Holland (a country he adored) and various cities in Germany and Italy. He stayed in boarding houses, in the districts where the Arab, Turkish and African immigrants lived, occasionally moving in with a lover, enjoying the idyll while it lasted, before walking out or being shown the door, and after each day's work in the street and drinks at a gay bar or a visit to a cinematheque with continuous screenings, Lorenzo (or Lorenza as he also liked to be called) would shut himself in his room to write and paint. For much of his life he lived alone. He was known to some as "the acrobatic hermit". His friends used to ask him how he wiped his arse after shitting, how he paid at the fruit shop, how he dealt with money, how he cooked. How, for God's sake, could he live on his own? Lorenzo answered all these questions and for almost every difficulty he had an ingenious solution. With a little ingenuity, my dear, you can find a way to do just about anything. If Blaise Cendrars, for instance, could out-box the best of them with one arm, Lorenza could clean her arse after shitting, and very nicely too.

In Germany, an intriguing but often eerie land, he bought himself a pair of prosthetic arms. They looked real and what he liked best was the way they made him feel like a robot or a cyborg in a science fiction film when he put them on and walked around. Seen from a distance, as he stepped out, for example, to meet a friend against a backdrop of violet sky, the visual effect was quite convincing. But he took them off when he worked in the street and the first thing he told his lovers, if they didn't know already, was that he had no arms. Some of them even liked him better that way.

Shortly before the historic Barcelona Olympics, an actor or actress or a whole theatre company from Catalonia toured in Germany and saw him perform in the street, or maybe in a small theatre, and mentioned him to the person who had been given the task of finding someone to represent Petra, Mariscal's cartoon character, the mascot or, to be more precise, the emblem of the Paralympics, which were to be held immediately after the Olympic Games. They say that when Mariscal saw Lorenzo leaping about in his skin-tight Petra costume like a schizophrenic principal from the Bolshoi Ballet, he said: the Petra of my dreams (which was typical: he doesn't waste words). When they talked afterwards, Mariscal was charmed and offered Lorenzo his studio so he could come to Barcelona to paint or write or whatever (which was typical of his generosity). But as it turned out, Lorenzo or Lorenza didn't need Mariscal's studio to put him on top of the world for the duration of the Paralympic Games. From the very first day he was a media favourite, doing a string of interviews, and it even looked as if he might eclipse Cobi, the Olympic mascot. At the time I was flat on my back with a clapped-out liver in the Valle Hebron Hospital in Barcelona, reading two or three newspapers a day, which is how I kept up with his exploits, jokes and anecdotes. Sometimes I had laughing fits reading the interviews. Sometimes they made me cry. I saw him on television too. He played his role very well.

Three years later, I found out he had died of AIDS. The person who told me wasn't sure if he had died in Germany or South America (he didn't know he was Chilean).

Sometimes, when I think of Stein and Soto, I can't help thinking of Lorenzo too.

Sometimes I think he was the best poet of the three. But usually I see them all together.

Although the only thing they had in common was having been born in Chile. And possibly a book: Stein may have read it; Soto certainly did (he mentioned it in a long article on exile and rootlessness published in Mexico), and Lorenzo devoured it enthusiastically, like almost every book he read. (How did he turn the pages? With his tongue: an example to us all!) The book was called *Ma Gestalt-thérapie*, and its author, Dr Frederick Perls, was a psychiatrist, a fugitive from Nazi Germany and a wanderer on three continents. As far as I know, it hasn't been published in Spain.

6

B ut let us return to the beginning, to Carlos Wieder and
the year of grace 1974.

At that time Wieder was at the height of his fame.
After his triumphant journey to Antarctica and aerial displays
over numerous Chilean cities, he was called upon to undertake
something grand in the capital, something spectacular to show
the world that the new regime and avant-garde art were not at
odds, quite the contrary.

Wieder was only too pleased to oblige. In Santiago he stayed
in Providencia, at the flat of a friend from the air force academy, and spent his days training at the Captain Lindstrom
airstrip, socialising at the military clubs and visiting friends at
their parents' houses, where he met or was more or less forcibly
introduced to their sisters, cousins and various young lady
friends, who were struck by his dashing appearance, his courteous and apparently shy manner, but also by his coldness, by
something remote in his gaze. As Pía Valle put it, there seemed
to be another pair of eyes behind his eyes. At night, free at last,
he devoted his time to the solitary preparation of a photographic

exhibition to be held in the flat, using the walls of the spare bedroom, which was to open on the same day as his display of aerial poetry.

Years later, the owner of the flat declared that he had not seen the photographs Wieder was planning to exhibit until the night of the opening. His first reaction to Wieder's project was naturally to offer him the living room, or the whole flat, to display the photos, but Wieder declined. He maintained that the photos required a restricted and well-defined space, such as the room that he, the photographer, was occupying. He said that after writing in the sky it would be appropriate – as well as charmingly paradoxical – to circumscribe the epilogue to his aerial poem within the bounds of the poet's den. As to the nature of the photos, according to the owner of the flat, Wieder wanted to surprise the guests, and would only say that it was visual poetry – experimental, quintessential, art for art's sake – and that everyone would find it amusing. He also made his host promise that neither he nor anyone else would go into the room until the night of the opening. The owner of the flat offered to dig out the key to the room so that Wieder could rest easy. But Wieder said that wouldn't be necessary; a promise was enough for him. So, solemnly, the owner of the flat gave his word of honour.

Naturally the invitations to the party in Providencia were limited to a select group: various pilots and young army officers (the oldest of them had not reached the rank of commander) who could reasonably be supposed to have a certain degree of aesthetic sensibility, a trio of journalists, two artists, an old right-wing, ex-avant-garde poet who seemed to have recovered his youthful vigour since the coup, a young society belle called Tatiana von Beck Iraola (apparently the only woman to attend the exhibition) and Carlos Wieder's father, who lived in Viña del Mar and was in delicate health.

Things got off to a bad start. On the morning of the air show, bulging black cumulus clouds came down the valley, heading south. Some of Wieder's superior officers advised him not to fly. He ignored the bad omens and apparently conferred with an unidentified individual in the dark corner of a hangar. Then he took off, and the spectators watched with more apprehension than admiration as he executed a few preliminary stunts. He did some hedge-hopping, then looped the loop right way up and upside down. But without releasing any smoke. The army men and their wives were enjoying the show, although some senior air force officers wondered what was really going on. Then the plane climbed and disappeared into the belly of an immense grey cloud that was moving slowly over the city as if it were guiding the black clouds of the storm.

Wieder travelled inside the cloud like Jonah inside the whale. For a while, the spectators awaited his thundering reappearance. A few began to get the uneasy feeling they had been tricked, left sitting there on makeshift stands at the Captain Lindstrom airstrip, staring at a sky that would yield only rain, not poetry. But most of them took advantage of the pause to get up from their seats, stretch their legs, mingle, greet friends or acquaintances, join the groups that kept forming and breaking up just as someone was about to chip in with a comment on the latest rumours, who'd been promoted to which position or the grave problems the nation was facing. The younger and livelier members of the crowd were gossiping about recent parties and who was going out with whom. Soon even Wieder's die-hard fans, rather than waiting in silence for the plane to reappear or reading all manner of omens in the blank sky, launched into down-to-earth discussions of everyday matters whose relevance to Chilean art or poetry was tenuous, to say the least.

Wieder's plane emerged far from the airstrip, over an outlying suburb of Santiago. There he wrote the first line: *Death is friendship*. Then he flew over some railway sheds and what appeared to be disused factories, although down in the streets he could make out people dragging cardboard boxes, children climbing on fences, dogs. To the left, at nine o'clock, he recognised two enormous shanty towns, separated by the railway tracks. He wrote the second line: *Death is Chile*. Then he swung round to three o'clock and headed for the city centre. Soon the river-like avenues appeared, the lattice of dull-hued snakes and ladders, the river itself, the zoo, the few high-rise buildings that were the city's pride. Seen from the air, as Wieder himself noted somewhere, a city is like a photo ripped into pieces, which, counter-intuitively, seem to scatter: a fragmentary, shifting mask. Over the presidential palace of La Moneda, he wrote the third line: *Death is responsibility*. Some pedestrians saw him: a beetle-like silhouette against the dark and threatening sky. Very few could decipher his words: the wind effaced them almost straight away. At one point someone tried to communicate with him by radio. Wieder didn't answer. On the horizon, at eleven o'clock, he saw the shapes of two helicopters approaching. He circled until they drew near, then shook them off in a second. On the way back to the airstrip he wrote the fourth and fifth lines: *Death is love* and *Death is growth*. When the strip came into sight, he wrote: *Death is communion*. But none of the generals or the generals' wives and children or the senior officers or the military, civil, ecclesiastical and cultural authorities present could read his words. An electric storm was building in the sky. From the control tower a colonel told him to hurry up and land. Wieder replied "Received", and immediately began to climb. For a moment those watching from below thought he was going to disappear into a cloud again. A captain, who was not in the official box, remarked that in Chile all poetic acts spelt disaster, usually just for individuals or families, but occasionally for the nation as a whole. Then came the lightning – the first bolt fell on the far side of Santiago, but was clearly visible from the stands at the Captain Lindstrom airstrip – and Carlos Wieder wrote: *Death is cleansing*, but so unsteadily, given the adverse weather conditions, that very few of the spectators, who by now had started to get up from their seats and open their umbrellas, could understand what had been written. All that was left in the sky were dark shreds, cuneiform characters, hieroglyphics, a child's scribble. The few who did manage to understand thought Carlos Wieder had gone mad. It started to rain and the crowd hurriedly dispersed. The cocktail party had to be shifted to a hangar, and by that stage, what with the delay and the downpour, everyone was in need of refreshment. In less than fifteen minutes all the canapés had been devoured. The waiters, recruits from the Quarter-master Corps, were amazingly quick on their feet and their diligence provoked the envy of some of the ladies present. Some of the officers discussed the aviator-poet's eccentric performance, but most of the conversations had moved on to questions of national (and even international) significance.

Meanwhile Carlos Wieder was still up in the sky, struggling with the elements. Beside the airstrip glistening with rain (the scene was worthy of a Second World War film) only a handful of friends remained, and two journalists who in their spare time wrote surrealist poems (or super-realist poems, as they preferred to say, aping a rather precious Spanish usage), their eyes fixed on the light plane veering around under the storm-clouds. Wieder himself was perhaps unaware that his public had so drastically diminished.

He wrote, or thought he wrote: *Death is my heart*. Then: *Take my heart*. And then his name: *Carlos Wieder*, undaunted by rain or lightning. Undaunted, above all, by incoherence.

And then he had no smoke left to write with (for some time it had looked as if the plane were on fire, or drawing out wisps of cloud, rather than sky-writing) but still he wrote: *Death is resurrection,* and the faithful who had stayed by the airstrip were bewildered, but they knew that Wieder was writing *something*. They understood or thought they understood the pilot's will, and they knew that although they couldn't make head or tail of it, they were witnessing a unique event, of great significance for the art of the future.

Then Carlos Wieder landed without the slightest difficulty (witnesses said he was sweating as if he had just emerged from a sauna) and was reprimanded by the officer from the control tower and certain other high ranking officers who were still wandering among the remnants of the cocktail party, and after drinking a beer without sitting down or talking to anyone (giving monosyllabic replies to every question), he went back to the flat in Providencia to prepare the second act of his Santiago gala.

The foregoing account of the air show may or may not be reliable. Or not. Perhaps the generals of the Chilean Air Force were not accompanied by their wives. Perhaps the Captain Lindstrom airstrip was never set up for a display of aerial poetry. It might be that Wieder wrote his poem in the sky over Santiago without asking permission or warning anyone, although it seems unlikely. Perhaps it didn't even rain that day in Santiago, although there are witnesses who, at the time, were sitting idle on park benches looking up at the sky or staring out of the windows of lonely rooms, and who still remember the words in the sky and the purifying rain that followed. But perhaps it all happened differently. In 1974, hallucinations were not uncommon.

The following account of the photographic exhibition in the flat is, however, accurate.

The first guests arrived at 9.00 in the evening. Most of them were old school friends who hadn't seen each other for some time. At 11.00, twenty people were present, all of them moderately drunk. No-one had yet entered the spare bedroom, occupied by

Wieder, on the walls of which were displayed the photos he was planning to submit to the judgment of his friends. Lieutenant Julio César Muñoz Cano, who years later was to publish a self-denunciatory memoir entitled *Neck in a Noose* relating his activities during the early years of the military regime, informs us that Carlos Wieder behaved normally (or perhaps *abnormally*: he was much quieter than usual, to the point of meekness, and throughout the night his face had a freshly washed look). He attended to the guests as if he were in his own home (everyone was getting along splendidly, too well, in fact, writes Muñoz Cano). Wieder was very pleased to see his friends from the air force academy, it had been such a long time; he had the good grace to comment on the morning's incidents without according them, or himself, any particular importance; he cheerfully tolerated the jokes (unsubtle at best and often in frankly poor taste) that are invariably told at such gatherings. Now and then he disappeared, shutting himself in the spare bedroom (and this time he did lock the door behind him), but he was never gone for long.

Finally, on the stroke of midnight, he climbed onto a chair in the living room, called for silence and said (these are his actual words according to Muñoz Cano) that it was time to plunge into the art of the future. He had changed back to the Wieder they knew: imperious, self-assured, his eyes somehow separate from his body, as if they were watching from another planet. Then he made his way to the door of the spare room and began to let them in one by one. One at a time gentlemen; the art of Chile is not for herds. According to Muñoz

Cano, he said this in a jocular tone of voice, looking at his father and winking first with his left eye, then with his right. As if he were a boy of twelve again, giving a secret sign. Calmly, Wieder senior smiled back at his son.

The first person to enter the room, logically enough since she was the only lady present and had a headstrong, impulsive temperament, was Tatiana von Beck Iraola. Tatiana, writes Muñoz Cano, came from an illustrious military family, and was, in her own slightly mad way, an independent woman, who always did as she pleased, went out with whom she fancied and held outrageous opinions, which were, in many cases, highly original if often contradictory. Years later she married a paediatrician, went to live in La Serena and had six children. In a passage whose melancholy tone is subtly tinged with horror, Muñoz Cano describes Tatiana as she was that night: a beautiful and confident young woman who went into the room expecting to see heroic portraits or boring photographs of the Chilean skies.

The room was lit in the usual way. There were no extra lamps or spotlights to heighten the visual effect of the photos. It was not meant to be like an art gallery, but simply a room, a spare bedroom temporarily occupied by a young visitor. There is, of course, no truth to the story that there were coloured lights or drum beats coming from a cassette player hidden under the bed. The ambience was meant to be everyday, normal, low-key.

Outside, the party continued. The young men drank as young men do, like the victors they were, and they held their drink like Chileans. The laughter, recalls Muñoz Cano, was contagious, without the slightest hint of menace or anything sinister. Somewhere a trio began to sing, arms around each other, one playing a guitar. Propped against the wall in groups of two or three, other guests talked about love or the future. They were all pleased to be there, at the aviator-poet's party; they were pleased with themselves and pleased to be friends of Carlos Wieder, although they weren't sure they quite understood him and were aware of the difference between him and themselves. The queue in the corridor kept breaking up; some guests had finished their drinks and went back for more, others got caught up in reaffirmations of eternal friendship and loyalty, a providential surge of fellow-feeling sweeping them back into the living room, from which they returned with flushed cheeks to take their places in the queue again. The smoke was thick, especially in the corridor. Wieder stood firm at the doorway. Two lieutenants were arguing and shoving each other (but gently) in the bathroom at the end of the passage. Wieder's father was one of the few who patiently kept his place in the queue. Muñoz Cano, as he admitted in his confession, kept pacing nervously back and forth, filled with foreboding. The two surrealist (or super-realist) reporters were talking with the owner of the flat. As he came and went, Muñoz Cano caught snatches of their conversation: travel, the Mediterranean, Miami, tropical beaches, fishing boats, voluptuous women.

Less than a minute after going in, Tatiana von Beck emerged from the room. She was pale and shaken – everyone noticed. She stared at Wieder as if she were going to say something to him but couldn't find the words. Then she tried to get to the bathroom, unsuccessfully. After vomiting in the passage, Miss von Beck staggered to the front door with the help of an officer who gallantly offered to take her home, although she kept saying she would prefer to go alone.

The second person to enter the room was a captain who had been one of Wieder's teachers at the academy. He remained inside. Wieder shut the door behind him (the captain had left it ajar) and stood there smiling, with an air of growing satisfaction. In the living room, some of the guests asked what on earth had got into Tatiana. She's just drunk, said a voice that Muñoz Cano didn't recognise. Someone put on a Pink Floyd record. How can you dance when there are no women? It's like a poofters' convention here, someone said. You're not supposed to dance to Pink Floyd, it's for listening, came the reply. The surrealist reporters whispered to each other. A lieutenant proposed they all go and find some whores straight away. Muñoz Cano says that at this point he felt as if they were outside, under the night sky, deep in the countryside, or at least that is how the voices sounded. In the hallway the atmosphere was even more tense. There was hardly any talking; it was like a dentist's waiting room. But who, wonders Muñoz Cano, has ever seen a dentist's waiting room where the *rotten teeth* (sic) are standing in line?

Wieder's father broke the spell. He made his way forward politely, addressing each officer by name as he excused himself, then went into the room. The owner of the flat followed him in. Almost immediately he came out again, went up to Wieder, seized him by the lapels, and for a moment it looked as if he would hit him, but then he turned away and stormed off to the living room in search of a drink. Now everyone, including Muñoz Cano, pressed into the bedroom or tried to. There they found the captain, sitting on the bed. He was smoking and reading some typed notes that he had torn off the wall. He seemed calm, although ash from his cigarette had dropped onto one of his trouser legs. Wieder's father was contemplating some of the hundreds of photos with which the walls and part of the ceiling had been decorated. A cadet who happened to be present, though what he was doing there no-one could explain (perhaps he was the younger brother of one of the officers) started crying and swearing and had to be dragged out of the room. The surrealist reporters looked disapproving but maintained their composure. Muñoz Cano claims to have recognised the Garmendia sisters and other missing persons in some of the photos. Most of them were women. The background hardly varied from one photo to another, so it seemed they had all been taken in the same place. The women looked like mannequins, broken, dismembered mannequins in some pictures, although Muñoz Cano could not rule out the possibility that up to thirty per cent of the subjects had been alive when the snapshots were taken. In general (according to Muñoz Cano) the photos were of poor quality, although they made an extremely vivid impression on all who saw them. The order in which they were exhibited was not haphazard: there was a progression, an argument, a story (literal and allegorical), a plan. The images stuck to the ceiling (says Muñoz Cano) depicted a kind of hell, but empty. Those pinned up in the four corners seemed to be an epiphany. An epiphany of madness. In other groups of photos the dominant mood was elegiac (but how, asks Muñoz Cano, could there be anything "nostalgic" or "melancholy" about them?) The symbols were few but telling. A photo showing the cover of a book by Joseph de Maistre: *St Petersburg Dialogues*. A photo of a young blonde woman who seemed to be dissolving into the air. A photo of a severed finger, thrown onto a floor of porous, grey cement.

After the initial hubbub, suddenly everyone fell silent. It was as if a high voltage current had run through the flat leaving us dumbstruck, says Muñoz Cano in a rare moment of lucidity. We stared at each other as if at strangers; our faces were still recognisable, of course, but different somehow, despicable and expressionless like the faces of sleepwalkers or idiots. Some guests left without saying good-bye, but among those who remained in the flat a peculiar atmosphere of camaraderie developed. And at that particularly delicate stage in the proceedings, a curious thing happened, adds Muñoz Cano: the telephone began to ring. Since the host failed to react, he answered it himself. An old man's voice asked for a certain Lucho Álvarez. Hello? Hello? Is Lucho Álvarez there, please? Instead of replying, Muñoz Cano handed the phone to the owner of the flat, who after an interminable pause asked, Does anyone know a Lucho Álvarez? The old man on the line, surmises Muñoz Cano, must have gone on talking or asking questions, possibly to do with this Lucho Álvarez. Nobody knew the caller. A few of the men let out absurdly high-pitched, nervous laughs. After listening in silence again for some time, the owner of the flat said, There's nobody here by that name, and hung up.

No-one was left in the room with the photos, except Wieder and the captain, and in the flat there were no more than eight people in all, according to Muñoz Cano, including Wieder's father, who didn't seem particularly disturbed (as if he were dutifully attending a cadets' party, which, for some reason that escaped him or was none of his business, had gone wrong). The owner of the flat, whom he had known since he was a boy, was avoiding his eye. The other survivors of the party were talking or whispering amongst themselves, but stopped when Wieder senior approached. He attempted to break the awkward silence by offering them drinks, hot or cold, and sandwiches, which he made in the kitchen, calmly, on his own. Don't worry, Mr Wieder, said one of the officers, looking at the ground. I'm not worried, Javierito, he replied. Just a hiccup in Carlos' career, that's all it'll be, said another. Wieder's father looked at him as if he didn't know what he was talking about. He was kind to us, recalls Muñoz Cano; he was on the edge of the abyss and he didn't know it, or he didn't care, or he was hiding it extra-ordinarily well.

Then Wieder emerged from the spare bedroom and went to talk with his father in the kitchen. No-one heard what they said, but they weren't in there for more than five minutes. When they reappeared, both had drinks in their hands. The captain also came out to get a drink, then shut himself in the room with the photos again, insisting that he was not to be disturbed. At his suggestion one of the lieutenants made a list of all the guests who had been present. Someone referred to an oath. Someone else started talking about discretion and the word of a gentleman and a soldier. A soldier's word, said a man who until then had seemed to be asleep. Another took offence and said the danger lay not with the soldiers but with the civilians, alluding to the pair of surrealist reporters. I'm sure our civilian friends know what's best for them, replied the captain. The surrealists hastened to agree, affirming that, as far as they were concerned, nothing had happened in the flat that night; they were men of the world, after all. Then someone made coffee, and some time later, but still quite a while before dawn, three men in uniform and one in civilian dress knocked at the front door and identified themselves as Military Intelligence agents. Those who had remained in the flat let them in, assuming they had come to arrest Wieder. At first, their presence inspired respect and a certain fear (especially on the part of the reporters), but as the minutes went by uneventfully, without a word from the agents, who were completely focussed on their work, the survivors of the party began to ignore them, as if they were servants who had come to clean up ahead of time. The agents shut themselves in the bedroom for what seemed an eternity with the captain and Wieder, one of whose friends wanted to go in and "give him moral support", but the agent in civilian dress told him not to be an idiot and to let them work in peace. Through the closed door, curses could be heard, the word "mad" repeated several times, and then only silence. Eventually the Intelligence agents left as quietly as they had arrived, carrying three shoe boxes provided by the owner of the flat, containing the photographs from the exhibition. Well, gentlemen, said the captain, before following them out, I advise you to get some sleep and forget everything that happened here tonight. A pair of lieutenants stood to attention, but the rest were too tired to observe protocol or any kind of ritual and they didn't even say good night (or good morning, since day was breaking). Just as the captain left, slamming the door behind him, Wieder emerged from the bedroom (the timing, had anyone been in a state to appreciate it, was worthy of a sit-com) and walked across the living room to the window, without so much as a glance at the others. He drew the curtains (it was still dark outside, but a faint glow could be seen in the distance, towards the Cordillera) and lit a cigarette. What happened, Carlos? asked Wieder's father. No answer. For a moment the silence seemed definitive, as if they had all fallen asleep on the spot, staring fixedly at Wieder's silhouette. The room, Muñoz Cano recalls, felt like a hospital waiting room. Finally the owner of the flat asked, Are you under arrest? I guess so, said Wieder, without turning to face them, looking out at the lights of Santiago, the sparsely scattered lights of Santiago. With painfully slow movements, as if he had to gather his courage, Wieder's father drew near and finally gave him a quick hug. Wieder did not respond. Why the drama? asked one of the surrealist reporters. You can shut up, said the owner of the flat. What do we do now? asked a lieutenant. Sleep it off, replied the host.

Muñoz Cano never saw Wieder again. But that last image was indelible: the big living room a mess; bottles, plates and overflowing ashtrays, a group of pale, exhausted men, and Carlos

Wieder at the window, showing no sign of fatigue, with a glass of whisky in his perfectly steady hand, contemplating the dark cityscape.

7

The reports of Carlos Wieder's activities from that night on are vague and contradictory. His shadowy figure makes a number of brief appearances in the shifting anthology of Chilean literature. According to some rumours, he was expelled from the air force at a secret court martial, held at night, which he attended in full-dress uniform, although his die-hard fans prefer to imagine him wearing a black greatcoat and a monocle, smoking a long pipe made from an elephant's tusk. The most unbalanced minds of his generation claim to have seen him wandering around Santiago, Valparaíso and Concepción, working at a variety of jobs and participating in strange artistic projects. He changed his name. He was associated with various ephemeral literary magazines, to which he contributed proposals for happenings that never happened, unless (and it hardly bears thinking about) he organised them in secret. A theatrical magazine published a short play in one act by a certain Octavio Pacheco, who was a mystery to everyone. This play is odd, to say the very least: the action unfolds in a world inhabited exclusively by Siamese twins, where sadism and masochism are children's games. Death is the only punishable offence in this world and the main subject of the twins' discussions throughout the work, along with non-being, nothingness and the next life. Each character devotes himself to torturing his Siamese twin for a certain period (a cycle, in the author's words), after which the tortured becomes the torturer and vice versa. But the inversion can only take place when "the depths have been plumbed". The reader of this play is, as one might imagine, confronted with every possible kind of cruelty. The action takes place in the principal characters' house and the car park of a supermarket where they encounter other Siamese twins who display a broad variety of disfiguring scars. Predictably, the play does not end with the death of one of the twins, but with a new cycle of pain. The thesis is somewhat simplistic: pain is our only connection with life; only pain can reveal what life is.

A university magazine published a poem called "The Zero Mouth". The poem, apparently a Latin-American travesty of Klebnikhov, was accompanied by three of the author's own sketches illustrating the "zero-mouth moment" (that is, the act of opening one's mouth as widely as possible to represent a zero or the letter O). Once again, the contribution was signed Octavio Pacheco, but Bibiano O'Ryan happened to discover a pamphlet box at the National Library containing the aerial poetry of Carlos Wieder as well as Pachecho's works for the theatre and texts signed in three or four other names, published in little magazines, some of which were marginal, low-budget affairs, while others were expensively produced and decently designed, with high-quality paper and abundant photographs (in one there were reproductions of almost all of Wieder's aerial poems, along with a complete chronology of his performances). The provenance of the magazines was diverse: Argentina, Uruguay, Brazil, Mexico, Colombia, Chile. The names suggested strategies rather than mere aspirations: *Hibernia, Germania, Storm, The Fourth Reich in Argentina, Iron Cross, Enough Hyperboles!* (a Buenos Aires fanzine), *Diphthongs and Synaloephae, Odin, Des Sängers Fluch* (with eighty per cent of the contributions in German, and, in No. 4, a "politico-artistic" interview with a certain K. W., a "Chilean science-fiction author", who partly reveals the plot of his forthcoming first novel), *Precision Strike, The Brotherhood, Poetry Pastoral & Urban* (a Colombian publication, and the only one of any interest: wild, destructive poetry by young, middle-class bikers, playing with drugs, crime and the symbols of the SS, as well as the prosody and theatricality of certain beat poets), *Martian Beaches, The White Army, Mister Pete* . . . Bibiano was flabbergasted. He thought he knew the Chilean literary scene inside out, but among the magazines in the box, there were at least seven published in Chile between 1973 and 1980 that he had never heard of. In one of them, *Sunflowers of Meat* (No. 1, April 1979), Wieder, under the pseudonym Masanobu (not, as one might be forgiven for thinking, a Samurai, but the Japanese painter Okumura Masanobu [1686-1784], discoursed on humour, the sense of the ridiculous, the atrocity of literary jokes, whether or not they draw blood, the private and the public grotesque, the laughable, gratuitous excess, and he concluded that no-one, *absolutely no-one*, had the right to pass judgment on the minor works that are born of mockery, develop through mockery and die in mockery. All writers are grotesque, writes Wieder. All writers are wretched, even those who come from well-to-do families, even Nobel Prize winners. Bibiano also came across a slender octavo volume, with a brown cover, entitled *Interview with Juan Sauer*. The book bore the imprint of The Fourth Reich in Argentina but gave no publisher's address or year of publication. It didn't take long to ascertain that Juan Sauer, who spoke in the interview about photography and poetry, was none other than Carlos Wieder. He replied to the interviewer's questions with long, wandering monologues, in which he sketched out a theory of art. Disappointing, according to Bibiano, as if Wieder, in a moment of weakness, were yearning for a normality he had never possessed, longing to be adopted as official poet by the Chilean state "in its capacity as guardian of culture". It was sickening: almost enough to make you believe the people who said they had seen Wieder selling socks and ties in Valparaíso.

For a while, whenever he got the chance, Bibiano checked the contents of that obscure pamphlet box in the library, always with consummate discretion. He soon discovered that new (although often disappointing) contributions kept being added. For a few days he thought he had found the key that would allow him to locate the elusive Carlos Wieder, but (as he confessed to me in a letter) he was scared, and his progress was so timid and circumspect as to be virtually indistinguishable from immobility. He wanted to find Wieder, he wanted to see him, but without being seen, and his worst nightmare was that one night Wieder might find *him*. Finally he overcame his fear and resolved to go to the library every day and wait. There was never a sign of Wieder. Bibiano decided to consult a librarian, a little old man whose chief occupation was gathering news about the lives and miraculous deeds of *every* Chilean writer, published or unpublished. He revealed to Bibiano that the person who supplemented the archive at irregular intervals was, in all probability, Wieder's father, who had retired to Viña del Mar and received copies of all his son's works by post. Spurred on by this revelation, Bibiano went back through the contents of the pamphlet box and came to the conclusion that some of the names he had assumed to be Wieder's pseudonyms were in fact nothing of the sort: they were real names, or invented ones, possibly, but invented by somebody else. Wieder was either deceiving his father with other people's creations, or his father was deceiving himself. Having reached this provisional conclusion (it was, Bibiano insisted, by no means definitive), which struck him as both sad and sinister, he decided that henceforth, for the sake of his emotional balance and physical safety, he would follow Wieder's career from a distance, without making any further attempt to approach him in person.

This he was able to do without difficulty. In certain literary circles, the legend of Carlos Wieder had spread like wildfire. Some said he had become a Rosicrucian, or that a group of Joseph Peladan's followers had tried to contact him, or that certain pages of *L'Amphithéâtre des sciences mortes* contained an encrypted prophecy or prediction of his momentous intervention "in the art and politics of a distant southern land". Some said he had taken refuge on the estate of an older woman, where he spent his days reading and taking photographs. Some said he occasionally appeared unannounced at the salon of Rebeca Vivar Vivanco, better known as Madame VV, an ultra-right-wing painter (for her, Pinochet and the generals were a spineless lot who would end up turning the Republic over to the Christian Democrats) and the driving force behind a series of artistic and military communes in the province of Aysén; she squandered one of the oldest family fortunes in Chile and was eventually confined to an asylum in the mid-80s (her wide-ranging works include new designs for the uniforms of the Chilean armed forces and a twenty-minute musical poem to be intoned by fifteen-year-old boys on the occasion of their ritual initiation into adult life, a ceremony which should take place, according to Madame VV, in the northern deserts, the snow-laden Cordillera or in the dark forests of the south, according to the boy's date of birth, the configuration of the planets, et cetera).

Towards the end of 1977, a new strategic war game appeared on the emerging national market and promptly disappeared again, in spite of a modest publicity campaign. The man behind this enterprise, according to those in the know (and Bibiano O'Ryan did not contradict them), was Carlos Wieder. The game covered the whole duration of the War of the Pacific, which broke out in 1879 between Chile and the alliance of Peru and Bolivia, each turn corresponding to a period of two weeks. More fun than Monopoly, claimed the advertising, although it was soon apparent to the players that there was a good deal more to the game than mere fun. On the surface it was a complex but classic war game, with a multiplicity of boards. On a second level, it became a magical exploration of the personalities and characters of the commanders. With the help of period photographs, the players were asked to ponder questions such as: could Arturo Prat have been the reincarnation of Jesus Christ? (The photo of Prat that came in the box did in fact bear a striking resemblance to certain images of Our Lord.) In which case, was the resemblance between Prat and Christ a "coincidence", a "symbol" or a "prophecy"? (Then the players were invited to consider the "real" meaning of events such as the boarding of the *Huascar*, the "real" significance of the fact that Prat's ship was called the *Esmeralda*, or the fact that both adversaries, the Chilean Prat and the Peruvian Grau, were actually Catalan.) There was, in addition, a third level to the game, which concerned the ordinary men who swelled the ranks of the victorious Chilean army as it marched undefeated to Lima, and the secret meeting that was held in a small underground church dating from colonial times, a meeting which, supposedly, marked the foundation (in the *Peruvian* capital) of what various authors with more or less stylistic felicity but a common sense of the absurd, have ventured to call the "Chilean Race". For the inventor of the game (probably Wieder), the Chilean Race was "founded" on a dark night in 1882, during Patricio Lynch's term as commander-in-chief of the occupying army. (There were also photos of Lynch, and a string of questions on subjects ranging from the meaning of his name to the secret reasons for certain campaigns he undertook both before and after his promotion to commander-in-chief. Why, for example, did the Chinese "adore" him?) How the game got past the censors and onto the market is a mystery; in any case it was a commercial failure and spelt doom for the manufacturers, who had to declare themselves bankrupt, although they had scheduled and announced the release of two more games by the same designer, one based on the wars against the Araucano Indians and the other, not really a war game, set in a city that bore a vague resemblance to Santiago, although it could also have been Buenos Aires (but bigger: a Mega-Buenos Aires or a Mega-Santiago), with a thriller-like scenario and a spiritual dimension, like *Escape from Colditz*, but exploring the mysteries of the soul and the human condition.

For some time Bibiano O'Ryan was obsessed with the two games that never saw the light of day. In one of his last letters to me he said he had contacted the largest private games library in the United States, in case either of them had been commercialised there. By return post he received a thirty-page catalogue of all the products in the war games category available in the United States over the previous five years. No trace of the Araucano game. As to the other one, about detectives in a Mega-Santiago, which was much harder to classify, they couldn't help at all.

Bibiano's investigations in the United States were not, however, limited to the world of board games. I heard from a friend (though I don't know if the story is true) that Bibiano contacted a member of the Philip K. Dick society in Glen Ellen, California, who was, for want of a better expression, a collector of literary curiosities. Apparently Bibiano entered into correspondence with this individual, who specialised in "secret messages in literature, painting, theatre and cinema", and told him the story of Carlos

Wieder. A specimen of that sort, the collector reckoned, was bound to wash up sooner or later in the United States. Bibiano's correspondent was called Graham Greenwood and like a true North American he had a firm and militant belief in the existence of evil, absolute evil. In his personal theology, hell was a framework or chain of coincidences. He explained serial killings as "explosions of chance". He explained the death of the innocent (and everything our minds refuse to accept) as the expression of chance set free. Fortune and Luck, he said, are the names of the devil's house. He appeared on local television stations and spoke on community radio up and down the west coast as well as in New Mexico, Arizona and Texas, promulgating his vision of crime. The way to fight evil, he said, was to learn how to read, and by this he meant not only words but numbers, colours, signs, arrangements of tiny objects, late-night and early-morning television shows, obscure films. He did not, however, believe in revenge: he was opposed to the death penalty and in favour of radical prison reform. He always carried a gun and defended the citizen's right to do so as the only way to prevent the rise of a fascist state. He did not limit the fight against evil to the planet Earth, which, in some of his cosmological rants resembled a penal colony. In space, he said, there are liberated zones, where chance cannot penetrate and the only source of pain is memory. The inhabitants of these zones are called angels, and their armies, legions. In a less literary but more radical way than Bibiano, Greenwood spent his time ferreting around in every weird underworld he could find. He had a wide range of friends: detectives, activists fighting for the rights of minority groups, feminists marooned in west coast motels, directors and producers who would never get a film off the ground and led lives as reckless and solitary as his own. The members of the Philip K. Dick Society, enthusiastic but discreet people as a rule, regarded him as a madman, but harmless and basically a good guy, as well as being a genuine expert on the works of Dick. For some time, Graham Greenwood kept an eye out for any traces that Wieder might have left in the United States, but he found nothing.

Meanwhile, Wieder's traces in the shifting anthology of Chilean poetry were becoming progressively fainter. A short-lived magazine published what appeared at first glance to be a shameless copy of a poem by Octavio Paz, signed "The Pilot". A reasonably prestigious Argentine periodical published a longer poem about a poet's gaze, a new kind of love and an old Indian maid fleeing a house in terror. This poem, according to the indefatigable Bibiano, referred to Amalia Maluenda, the Garmendia sisters' Mapuche maid, who had vanished along with her employers, although members of a team set up by the Catholic Church to investigate the disappearances claimed to have seen her in the vicinity of Mulchén or Santa Bárbara, on a ranch in the foothills of the Cordillera, where she was living under the protection of her nephews, having sworn never to speak to white people again. The poem (Bibiano sent me a photocopy) was certainly intriguing, but it proved nothing, and may not even have been written by Wieder.

Everything seemed to suggest that he had turned his back on literature.

Nevertheless his work lived on, precariously, desperately (as he would have wished, perhaps), yet it lived on. A handful of young men read it, reinvented him, tried to become his followers, but how can you follow someone who is not moving, someone who is trying, with every appearance of success, to become invisible?

Finally Wieder left Chile behind, along with the little magazines in which he had published his last, half-hearted creative efforts, imitations that left the reader wondering why, signed with his initials or improbable pseudonyms. He disappeared, but his physical absence (in fact he had *always* been an absent figure) did not put an end to the speculations, the passionate and contradictory readings to which his work gave rise.

When the followers of the critic Ibacache gathered after his cremation in 1986, a letter turned up, presumably sent by some-one close to Wieder, announcing the death of the aviator-poet. The existence of this letter soon became public knowledge. It referred vaguely to literary executors, but Ibacache's circle of friends, eager not to have their names or that of the deceased sullied in any way, closed ranks and declined to reply. According to Bibiano, the news of Wieder's death was false, and was probably invented by Ibacache's cronies themselves, who were following their master into dementia.

Shortly afterwards, however, Wieder featured prominently in a posthumous volume by Ibacache entitled *What the Writers Read*. This exercise in anecdote and name-dropping, possibly apocryphal in content and supposedly light-hearted in tone, purported to record the desert-island choices of authors whom Ibacache had favoured with fervent or indulgent commentaries in the course of his protracted career. It was composed of observations on the reading habits – and bookshelves – of such writers as Huidobro (surprising), Neruda (predictable), Nicanor Parra (Wittgenstein and Chilean folk poetry: Parra was probably pulling his leg, or was it Ibacache's joke on the reader?), Rosamel del Valle, Díaz Casanueva, and others, with the notable exception of Enrique Lihn, who was a sworn enemy of the Catholic critic and antique collector. Of the younger writers, the youngest was Carlos Wieder, and this was an indication of the hopes Ibacache had pinned on him. In the section devoted to Wieder's readings, the critic's style, usually full of the flourishes and generalities that are the stock in trade of the pompous literary journalist (which is what, at bottom, he had always been), underwent a gradual, in fact a perfectly smooth, transformation, losing the festive and familiar tone of the sections in which he had dealt with his other idols, friends or followers. Alone in his study, Ibacache tried to bring Carlos Wieder into focus. Calling on all the resources of his memory, he strove to recapture Wieder's voice and spirit, the face he had imagined during a long telephone conversation one night; but he failed, and his miserable failure was evident in the style of his notes, veering from jaunty to pedantic (which is not uncommon in Latin American criticism), then from pedantic to melancholy and perplexed. Wieder's favourite authors, as recorded by Ibacache, are a varied lot, although the list may tell us more about the critic's erratic and out-of-step preferences: Heraclitus, Empedocles, Aeschylus, Euripides, Simonides, Anacreon, Callimachus, Honestus of Corinth. Ibacache allowed himself a dig at Wieder, betting that his bedside table was burdened with the *Palatine Anthology* and the *Anthology of Chilean Poetry* (though perhaps, on second thoughts, this was not a joke). He pointed out that Wieder – whose voice at the other end of the telephone line sounded like wind and rain, and this, from a man who collected antiques, should be taken literally – knew the *Dialogue of a Man with His Soul* and had made a careful study of *'Tis Pity She's a Whore* by John Ford, whose complete works, including those written in collaboration, he had annotated in detail. (Ever the sceptic, Bibiano thought it more likely that Wieder's familiarity with Ford was limited to the Italian film based on his best known play, which came out in Latin America in 1973 or thereabouts, and whose main and perhaps sole redeeming feature was the presence of a young and hauntingly beautiful Charlotte Rampling.)

The fragment concerning the erudition of the "promising poet Carlos Wieder" broke off abruptly, as if Ibacache had suddenly realised he was stepping into a void.

But there was more to come: in an article about seaside cemeteries on the Pacific coast, a rambling, sentimental piece, republished in a volume entitled *Etchings and Watercolours*, between discoursing on a cemetery near Las Ventanas and another in the vicinity of Valparaíso, for no apparent reason Ibacache described night falling in a nameless village, an empty square where long shadows flickered and trembled, and a silhouette, the silhouette of a young man wearing a trench coat, and a scarf or cravat around his neck, which partly hid his face. Ibacache and the stranger talked, but between them lay a strip or rectangle of lamplight, which neither dared to cross. In spite of the distance, their voices carried clearly. Although the general tone of the exchange was civilised and the stranger had a pleasant-sounding voice, occasionally he lapsed into coarse or violent language. The meeting, being strictly confidential in nature, came to an end when a pair of lovers appeared in the square, followed by a dog (it might as well have been a pair of policemen on the beat). They were gone again in the space of a breath or the wink of an eye, but so was the stranger, who disappeared into the shadows and the unkempt greenery of the square, leaving Ibacache leaning on his stick, meditating on the inscrutable ways of destiny. Was it Wieder? Or a figment of the critic's imagination? Who knows.

In spite of the rumours of his death and the lack of evidence to the contrary, rather than sinking into oblivion with the passing years Wieder became a mythic figure and his alleged ideas found a following. Certain enthusiasts set off into the wide world intending, if not to bring him back to Chile, at least to have their photos taken with the great man. But all their efforts were in vain. They lost track of him in South Africa, Germany or Italy . . . After a long pilgrimage (or several months of tourism, according to the cynics) the young men returned from their quests penniless and empty-handed.

Carlos Wieder's father, presumably the one person who knew his whereabouts, died in 1990. And nobody came to visit his recess in a neglected corner of the Valparaíso municipal cemetery.

As the years went by it was gradually supposed in Chilean

literary circles that Carlos Wieder was dead too, a reassuring thought for many, as times began to change.

In 1992 his name appeared prominently in a judicial report on torture and the disappearance of prisoners. It was the first time he had come to public notice in a non-literary context. In 1993 he was linked to an "independent operational group" responsible for the death of various students in and around Concepción and Santiago. In 1994 a collective of Chilean journalists published a book about the disappearances in which he was again mentioned. In the same year, Muñoz Cano, who had left the air force, published his memoir, one chapter of which described the photographic exhibition in the Providencia flat: a detailed account, though marred in places by the excessive intensity and nervous agitation of the prose. A few years earlier, an obscure press specialising in small-format poetry books had published Bibiano O'Ryan's *The Warlocks Return*. The book was a success and the print runs soon outstripped the publisher's fondest dreams. *The Warlocks Return* is a highly readable study of fascist literary movements in South America from 1972 to 1989 (stylistically, it owes something to the detective novels Bibiano and I used to devour during our years in Concepción). Among the enigmatic and extravagant characters who crowd the pages of the book, by far the most imposing is Carlos Wieder; he alone stands out clearly from the vertigo and babble of those accursed decades. He is (as I'm afraid we say in Latin America) a shining example. In the chapter devoted to Wieder (the longest in the book), entitled "Exploring the Limits", Bibiano relinquishes his generally measured and objective tone, and evokes the shining of the example in question; it is as if he were retelling a horror film. At one point, rather inappropriately, he even compares the story of Wieder to William Beckford's *Vathek*, quoting Borges' commentary on that work: "I would go so far as to affirm that it is the first truly atrocious Hell in literature." Bibiano's account of Wieder and his poetics is faltering, as if the presence of the aviator-poet had disturbed and disoriented him. Oddly, although he is quite at ease with Argentine or Brazilian torturers and even makes fun of them, when faced with Wieder, he becomes tense, accumulates adjectives ineptly and indulges in scatology, as if he were trying not to blink, not to let his subject (Carlos Wieder the pilot, Ruiz-Tagle the autodidact) disappear over the horizon. But everyone blinks in the end, even writers, especially writers, and, as always, Wieder vanishes.

Only three former comrades spoke out in the lieutenant's defence. All three were retired and all three were prompted by a passion for truth and a concern for the common good. The first, a major in the army, said that Wieder was a sensitive and refined individual; in his own way, he was yet another victim of those dark years during which the destiny of the Republic hung in the balance. The second, a sergeant from Military Intelligence, spoke in plainer terms of Wieder as an energetic, good-humoured and hard-working young man (which was more than you could say for some of them), who treated his men decently, not like sons exactly, because most of us were older than he was, more like younger brothers. My little brothers, Wieder used to call them, for no apparent reason, while a broad smile spread across his face (what was he so happy about?).

Wieder's third defender, an officer who had accompanied him on a number of missions in Santiago – a small number, as he was quick to point out – affirmed that Air Force Lieutenant Wieder had only done his duty as a Chilean: what other Chileans should have done, or had tried to do but could not. Prisoners are a dead weight in times of civil war. Such was the maxim that had guided Wieder and several of his colleagues, and with the nation in the throes of that catastrophe, who could blame them for overstepping the bounds of duty? Sometimes, he added pensively, finishing off a prisoner is more an act of kindness than a punishment: "What you have to understand is that Carlitos Wieder looked down on the world as if he were standing on top of a volcano; he saw you and me and himself from a great height, and, in his eyes, we were all, to be quite frank, pathetic insects. That is how he was; he believed that Nature intervenes actively in history, shaping it, buffeting our lives, although in our pitiful ignorance we usually attribute these blows to bad luck or destiny."

Finally, a courageous and pessimistic judge indicted Wieder in a case that would never get very far. The defendant, of course, did not appear for the trial. Another judge, in Concepción this time, named him as the prime suspect in the murder of Angelica Garmendia and the disappearance of her sister and aunt. Amalia Maluenda, the Mapuche maid, made a surprise appearance in the witness box and her presence kept the journalists busy for a week. Over the years her Spanish had dwindled. When she spoke in court, every second word was in Mapuche, and the two young Catholic priests who escorted her like bodyguards, never leaving her alone for a moment, had to serve as interpreters. In her memory, the night of the crime was one episode in a long history of killing and injustice. Her account of the events was swept up in a cyclical, epic poem, which, as her dumbfounded listeners came to realise, was partly her story, the story of the Chilean citizen Amalia Maluenda, who used to work for the Garmendias, and partly the story of the Chilean nation. A story of terror. When she spoke of Wieder, she seemed to be talking about several different people: an invader, a lover, a warrior, a demon. When she spoke of the Garmendia sisters, she likened them to the air, to garden plants or puppies. Remembering the black night of the crime, she said she had heard the music of the Spanish. When asked to clarify what she meant by "the music of the Spanish", she replied: "Rage, sir, sheer, futile rage."

None of the cases made much headway. The country had too many problems to concern itself for long with the fading figure of a serial killer who had disappeared years ago.

Chile forgot him.

8

This is where Abel Romero appears on the scene and I make my reappearance. Chile had forgotten us as well.

During the time of Allende, Romero had been something of a celebrity in the police force. Now he was in his fifties: short, dark, all skin and bone, his black hair slicked back with brilliantine or gel. His owed his modest fame to two cases, which had, as the saying goes, rocked the nation, or at least the readers of the crime reports. The first was a murder (or, according to Romero, a puzzle). The scene was a boarding-house on the Calle Ugalde in Valparaíso. The victim was found shot in the forehead; the door of the room was bolted and jammed shut from the inside with a chair. The windows had also been shut from the inside, besides which anyone trying to escape that way would have been seen from the street. Since the weapon was found beside the dead man's body, the case was initially treated, logically enough, as a suicide. But the forensic reports soon revealed that the victim had not fired the weapon. The dead man's name was Pizarro, and as far as anyone knew he had no enemies. He led a quiet, rather solitary life and had no occupation or means of earning a living, although it was later discovered that he received a monthly allowance from his wealthy family in the south. The newspapers took up this curious case: how had the killer got out of the victim's room? Experiments with the doors of the other rooms showed that it was virtually impossible to shoot the bolt from the outside. As for shooting the bolt and jamming the door shut with a chair against the handle, it was simply inconceivable. Tests on the windows revealed that, one in ten times, if they were shut from the outside with a quick, firm action, the clasp fell into place. But only a tight-rope walker could have escaped from there, and, besides, the window was in full view of the street below, which was normally very busy at the time the murder took place. Nevertheless, in the end, for want of a plausible alternative, the police concluded that the killer had escaped through the window, and the national press nicknamed him the "tight-rope walker". Then Romero was sent down from Santiago, and he solved the mystery in twenty-four hours. After a further eight hours of interrogation (in which Romero had no part), the killer signed a confession that coincided almost exactly with the detective's deductions.

The story, as Romero told it to me years later, went like this: Pizarro, the victim, had dealings of some kind with his landlady's son, a certain Enrique Martínez Corrales, also known as Enriquito or Henry, who was often to be seen at the Viña del Mar racecourse, a place which, according to Romero, inevitably attracted the local low-life and those afflicted with "the black vein of destiny", as Victor Hugo wrote in *Les Misérables*, the only "masterpiece of world literature" that Romero admitted to having read in his youth, although unfortunately with the passing of the years he had forgotten it completely except for Javert's suicide (I will return to *Les Misérables* shortly). Enriquito, who was apparently deep in debt, somehow got Pizarro involved in his business dealings. For as long as Enriquito's run of bad luck lasted, the pair stuck together and their adventures were unwittingly financed by the victim's parents. But one day fortune began to smile on the landlady's son and he gave his friend the slip. Pizarro felt he had been hard done by. They argued, exchanged threats, and one day at noon Enriquito came to Pizarro's room armed with a pistol. He only meant to frighten him, but at the climactic moment, as he was pointing the gun at Pizarro's head, it accidentally went off. What could he do? In the midst of this nightmare come true, Enriquito had his one and only brilliant idea. He knew that if he simply disappeared, he would soon be the prime suspect. He knew that if Pizarro's murder was left unembellished, they would soon be on his trail. He needed, therefore, to clothe it in mystery and strangeness. He closed the door from the inside, used a chair to jam it shut, put the pistol in the dead man's hand, checked the windows, and as soon as he was satisfied with this suicide scene, he got into the wardrobe and waited. He knew his mother and the other boarders would be eating or watching television in the living room; he was confident they would break down the door without waiting for the police. And sure enough, they came bursting in, and Enriquito, who had not even closed the wardrobe door, slipped quietly out and joined the group of boarders gaping in horror at Pizarro's body. A very straight forward case, said Romero, but it made me famous, undeservedly, and I had to pay for it dearly later on.

The case that really made him a household name, however, was a kidnapping at Las Cármenes, an estate near Rancagua, a few months before the military coup. It involved Cristóbal Sánchez Grande, one of the country's richest businessmen, who had disappeared, kidnapped, it seemed, by a leftist organisation, which had contacted the government demanding an exorbitant sum for the release of the hostage. For weeks the police didn't know what to do. Romero was in charge of one of three teams conducting the search, and it occurred to him that Sánchez Grande might have simulated his own kidnapping. They tailed a young man from the right-wing group Patria y Libertad for several days, and in the end he lowered his guard and led them to the Las Cármenes estate. While half the men surrounded the house, Romero had three officers take up positions as snipers; then, with a pistol in each hand and accompanied by a youngster called Contreras, who was the bravest of the lot, he went in and arrested Sánchez Grande. In the shoot-out, two of the Patria y Libertad thugs protecting the businessman were killed and Romero was wounded along with one of the policemen covering the back of the house. This operation earned Romero the Bravery Medal, awarded by Allende in person. Professionally, it was the high point of his life, a life that had been, as he put it himself, richer in disappointment than in happiness.

Naturally I remembered who he was. He had been a celebrity. His name used to appear in the crime reports (were they before or after the sports section?) in connection with places we considered shameful (but what did we know about shame back then?), settings for third-world crime in the '60s and '70s: shacks, vacant lots, dimly-lit country houses. And Allende had personally awarded him the Bravery Medal. I lost the medal, he told me sadly, and now I don't even have a photo to prove it, but I remember the ceremony as if it was yesterday. He still looked like a policeman.

After the coup he was imprisoned for three years and when he got out he went to Paris, where he took any work he could find. From the little he said about those first years in France, I gathered he had done everything from bill posting to waxing office floors at night, when the buildings are closed, a job that gives you plenty of time to think. The mysterious bureaux of Paris. That's how he referred to the night-bound office buildings, when all the floors are dark except for one, and then the lights go off, before another floor lights up, and so on. From time to time, if a nocturnal passer-by or a bill poster stopped to watch, he would see a figure at the window of one of those empty buildings, smoking or gazing out over the city, hands on hips: one of the night cleaners.

Romero was married; he had a son and was planning to return to Chile and start a new life.

When I asked him why he had come to see me (by this stage I had already invited him in and put on the kettle for a cup of tea), he said he was trying to track down Carlos Wieder.

Bibiano O'Ryan had given him my address in Barcelona. Do you know Bibiano? Not personally, he said. I wrote him a letter and he replied; then we talked on the phone. Just like Bibiano, I said, wondering how long it had been since I'd seen him: almost twenty years. He's a good man, your friend, said Romero, and although he seems to know a great deal about Mr Wieder, he thinks you know more. That's not true, I said. There's money in it, said Romero, if you help me find him. And he looked around the flat as if he were calculating my price. I didn't think he'd press his luck, so I decided to keep quiet and wait. I poured the tea. He took it with milk and seemed to enjoy it. Sitting there at my table he seemed much smaller and thinner than he really was. I can offer you two hundred thousand pesetas, he said. All right, I replied, but how can I help you?

By advising me on poetic matters, he said. This was his reasoning: Wieder was a poet, I was a poet, he was not. To find a poet, he needed the help of another poet.

I told him that in my opinion Carlos Wieder was a criminal, not a poet. All right, all right, let's not be intolerant, said Romero. Maybe in Wieder's opinion, or anyone else's for that matter, *you're* not a poet, or you're a bad one, and he's the real thing. It all depends on the glass we see through, as Lope de Vega said, don't you think? Two hundred thousand in cash, right now? I asked. Two hundred thousand pesetas straight up, he said briskly, but remember that from now on, you're working for me and I want results. How much are *you* getting paid? I asked. Enough, he said. My client isn't short of money.

The next day, he came to my flat with fifty thousand

pesetas in an envelope and a suitcase full of literary magazines. I'll give you the rest when my payment comes through,
he said. I asked why he thought Carlos Wieder was still alive.
Romero smiled to himself (he had a smile like a weasel or a
field mouse) and said it was his client who thought Wieder
was still alive. And what makes you think he's in Europe and
not in America or Australia? I know his profile, he said. Then
he invited me to lunch at a restaurant in the Calle Tallers, the
street my flat was in (he was staying in a reasonably priced,
respectable boarding-house in the Calle Hospital, a stone's
throw away), and the conversation turned to his years in Chile,
the country as we remembered it, and the Chilean police force,
which Romero (to my astonishment) regarded as one of the
finest in the world. You're a fanatic and a chauvinist, I said
to him over dessert. Not at all, he replied. When I was in
Criminal Investigations, there was no such thing as an un-
solved murder case. And the boys who went into Investigations
were well educated; they'd all finished secondary school with
good marks, then they had three years in the academy with
excellent teachers. I remember the criminologist González
Zavala, Doctor González Zavala, God rest his soul, saying that
the two best police forces in the world, at least as far as homicide was concerned, were the British and the Chilean. I told
him not to make me laugh.

We left the restaurant at four o'clock in the afternoon, having drunk two bottles of wine with our meal. Good convivial
Spanish wine, better than French, said Romero. I asked him if
he had something against the French. A shadow seemed to pass

over his face and he said no, he was ready to leave, that was all; he had been living in France for too long.

We had coffee at the Céntrico and talked about *Les Misérables*. For Romero, Jean Valjean, who reappears first as Madeleine, then as Fauchelevent, was an everyday character, the sort of character you might come across in the chaotic cities of Latin America. Javert, by contrast, struck him as exceptional. He's like a session with a psychoanalyst, Romero said. It was immediately clear to me that he had never undergone psychoanalysis, although it was a form of treatment for which he had the highest regard. He felt compassion and admiration for Hugo's policeman Javert, and that's why the character seemed like an indulgence, "a treat to be reserved for special occasions". I asked him if he had seen the film, the old French version. No, he said. I know there's a musical playing in London, but I haven't seen that either; it's probably like Gilbert and Sullivan. As I said, he didn't remember the plot at all, except that Javert kills himself. I had my doubts. Maybe in the film he doesn't. (Trying to remember the film, only two images come back to me: the barricades in 1832 with the student revolutionaries and *gamines* bustling around, and the figure of Javert after he has been rescued by Valjean, standing in the mouth of a sewer, gazing at the horizon, while sewage plunges into the Seine making a truly magnificent sound, like a cataract . . . although I'm probably mixing it up with another film.) These days, said Romero, savouring the last drops of a coffee with cognac, the policeman gets divorced, and that's it, at least in American films. But Javert killed himself. Times have changed, eh?

Then we climbed the five floors to my flat, where he opened the suitcase and put the magazines on the table. Take your time, he said. While you're reading, I'll go and do a bit of sightseeing. Which museums would you recommend? I remember I told him roughly how to get to the Picasso Museum and from there to the Sagrada Familia, and off he went.

I didn't see him again for three days.

The magazines he left were all European. They came from Spain, France, Portugal, Italy, England, Switzerland and Germany. There were two from Romania as well, one from Poland and one from Russia. Most were fanzines printed in small numbers. A few of the French, German and Italian publications looked professional and must have had solid financial backing, but the rest were home-made jobs, photocopied or even mimeographed (one of the Romanian magazines), and it certainly showed: the poor reproduction, cheap paper and inept design matched the gutter-like content. I leafed through them all. According to Romero, somewhere, in one of them, there should have been a contribution by Wieder, under a pseudonym, of course. They were not the usual sort of right-wing literary magazines: four were the work of skinhead groups, two were brought out irregularly by football fans, at least seven were mainly given over to science fiction, three were offshoots of war games clubs, four (two Italian and two French) were devoted to the occult and one of these (in Italian) openly advocated devil worship, at least fifteen were clearly sympathetic to Nazism, six were associated with the pseudo-historical "revisionist" movement (three French, two Italian and one from French-speaking

Switzerland), one, the Russian magazine, was a chaotic mixture of all the aforementioned tendencies, or at least that was the conclusion I reached after examining the caricatures (of which there were an inordinate number, as if the potential readers had become illiterate, luckily for me, since I can't read Russian), and almost all of them were racist and anti-Semitic.

It wasn't until the second day of reading that I started to get really interested. I was living on my own, had no money and was in pretty poor health. None of my work had been published anywhere for ages, and for a while I hadn't even been writing. My lot in life seemed miserable. I think I had begun to make a habit of self-pity. Romero's magazines piled up on the table (I took to eating over the sink so as not to disturb them), arranged according to nationality, date of publication, political orientation or literary genre, worked on me like a kind of antidote. After two days of reading I felt physically ill, but this, I soon realised, was due to lack of sleep and proper food, so I went out and had a cheese roll, then put myself to bed. When I woke up six hours later, I felt refreshed and ready to go on reading or re-reading (or guessing, depending on the language of the magazine). I was gradually being drawn into the story of Carlos Wieder, which was also the story of something more – exactly what I couldn't tell – but one night I had a dream about it. I dreamt I was travelling in a big wooden boat, a galleon perhaps, crossing the Great Ocean. There was a party on the poop deck and I was there, writing a poem, or perhaps writing in my diary, and looking at the sea. Then an old man, on a yacht, not the galleon, or standing on a breakwater, started shouting "Tornado! Tornado!" just like the scene from *Rosemary's Baby*, the Polanski film. At that point the galleon began to sink and all the survivors were cast adrift on the sea. I saw Carlos Wieder, clinging to a barrel of brandy. I was clinging to a rotten spar. And only then, as the waves pushed us apart, did I understand that Wieder and I had been travelling in the *same boat*; he may have conspired to sink it, but I had done little or nothing to stop it going down. When Romero returned, after three days, I was very glad to see him.

He hadn't been to the Picasso Museum or the Sagrada Familia, but he had visited the Nou Camp Museum and the new aquarium. The first time I'd seen a shark close up like that, he said. Quite something, I tell you. When I asked him what he thought of the Nou Camp, he said he had always considered it the finest stadium in Europe. Pity Barcelona lost last year against Paris Saint-Germain. You're not going to tell me you're a *culé*, are you, Romero? He wasn't familiar with the word. I explained its origin and he was amused. Then he seemed to drift off for a while. Here I'm a *culé*, he said. Barcelona's my favourite European team, but in my heart I'll always be a Colo-Colo supporter. What can you do? he added sadly and proudly.

That afternoon, after lunch at a bar in Barceloneta, he asked me if I'd read the magazines. I'm working through them, I replied. The next day he turned up with a television and a video player. These are for you, a gift from my client. What do you think? I don't watch television, I said. Well you should, you don't know what you're missing. I hate game shows, I said. Some of them are very interesting, said Romero. Simple people, auto-didacts taking on the world. I remembered that Carlos Wieder was an autodidact, or pretended to be, all those years ago in Concepción. I read books, Romero, I said, and magazines too now, and sometimes I write. And it shows, said Romero. I don't mean that as an insult, he added immediately, I've always respected priests and writers who renounce worldly possessions. I saw a film with Paul Newman once, he said. He was a writer and they gave him the Nobel Prize and then he confessed that for years he'd been writing detective novels under a pseudonym to earn his living. I respect that sort of writer. You can't have known many, I remarked. Romero didn't notice the sarcasm. You're the first, he said. Then he explained that he couldn't really set up the television in the boarding-house where he was staying and told me I should watch the three videos he had brought. I think I laughed out of sheer fright. I said, Don't tell me you've got Wieder on film? I have indeed, on these three tapes, said Romero.

We set up the television, and before plugging in the video player Romero tried to get one of the local channels, unsuc-cessfully. You'll have to buy an antenna, he said. Then he put in the first video. I stayed where I was, sitting at the table cov-ered with magazines. Romero sat down in the one and only armchair.

They were low-budget pornographic films. Halfway through the first one (Romero had brought a bottle of whisky and he was taking little swigs as he watched) I confessed that I couldn't take three porno films in a row. Romero waited till the end then switched off the video. Watch them tonight, on your own, no hurry, he said as he put the whisky bottle away in a corner of the kitchen. Am I supposed to recognise him? Is he one of the actors? I asked as he was leaving. Romero smiled enigmatically. The magazines are the main thing; the films are just an idea I had, for the sake of thoroughness.

That night I watched the two remaining films, then I went back and watched the first one again. And then I watched the other two a second time. Wieder didn't appear in any of them. And Romero didn't turn up the next day. I thought the films must have been one of his jokes. Yet within the four walls of my flat, Wieder's presence kept growing stronger, as if in some way the films had conjured him up. At one point Romero had told me there was no need to dramatise things, but I could feel my whole life being sucked into the sewer.

When Romero returned he was sporting a new suit, fresh off the peg, and he had brought me a gift. Fervently hoping it would not be an item of clothing, I opened the packet. It contained a novel by García Márquez – which I'd already read, though I didn't tell him that – and a pair of shoes. Try them on, he said. I hope they're the right size. The French are very keen on Spanish shoes. To my surprise, they fitted me perfectly.

Explain the riddle of the porno films, I said. You didn't notice anything strange or out of the ordinary, nothing that struck you as odd? asked Romero. From his tone of voice I could tell he didn't give a damn about the films, the magazines, or anything at all, except perhaps returning to Chile with his family.

All I know is that I'm becoming more and more obsessed with this bastard Wieder, I said. And is that a good thing or a bad thing? It's not funny, Romero, I said. All right, I'm going to tell you a story, said Romero. The lieutenant is there in all three films, but *behind* the camera. So Wieder directed them? No, said Romero, he was the cameraman.

Then he told me about a crew that used to make pornographic films in a villa on the Gulf of Tarento. One morning, it must have been a couple of years before, they were all found dead. Six people in all: three actresses, two actors and a cameraman. The prime suspect was the director-producer, who was taken into custody. They also arrested the owner of the villa, a lawyer from Corigliano who was associated with the underworld of violent hard-core: pornographic films showing real criminal acts. Both had alibis and had to be released. After a while the case was shelved. And what did Carlos Wieder have to do with all this? There was a second cameraman. A certain R. P. English. And the Italian police had never been able to track him down.

Were Wieder and English one and the same? Romero thought so when he began his investigation, and for some time he travelled around Italy looking for people who had encountered English, showing them a photo of Wieder (the one in which he is posing next to his plane), but everyone he talked to seemed to have forgotten the cameraman, as if he had never existed or had no face to remember. Finally, in a clinic in Nîmes, he found an actress who recalled having worked with English. The actress was called Joanna Silvestri and she was stunning, said Romero, the most beautiful woman I've ever seen, I swear. More beautiful than your wife? I asked, to tease him a bit. Oh, my wife's getting on now, she doesn't count, said Romero. Nor do I, he added almost straightaway. Anyway, she was the most beautiful woman I'd ever seen. What I really mean is, the prettiest. You have to take your hat off to a woman like that, believe me. I asked him to describe her. Tall, blonde, with something in her gaze that made you feel like a child again. Something soft like satin, but with flashes of sadness and determination. She also had wonderful bones and very pale skin, with that olive undertone you often see in Mediterranean countries. A woman to day-dream about, but also to share your life with, the good times and the bad. You could tell, said Romero, from her bones, her skin, the depth of her gaze. I never saw her standing up, but I imagine she would have looked like a queen. The clinic wasn't luxurious, but it had a little garden, where the patients used to go and sit in the afternoon. Most of them were French or Italian. The last time I went to see her, I suggested after a while that we go down there together (perhaps I was afraid she would get bored alone with me in the room). She said she couldn't. We were talking in French, but now and then she would lapse into Italian. She looked me in the eye and said, I can't, in Italian, and I tell you I felt like the most helpless, useless, miserable man in the world. I don't know how to explain it: I thought I was going to burst into tears. But I controlled myself and tried to go on talking about the investigation I was supposed to be conducting. She thought it was funny that a Chilean was

looking for a man called English. The Chilean detective, she
said with a smile. She looked like a cat, propped up on the
pillows, with her arms crossed. And the shape of her legs under
the blankets . . . even that was like a miracle, I don't mean the
sort that leaves you dazed, but a miracle simple as the day,
that leaves you feeling peaceful, more peaceful than before.
Christ Almighty, she was gorgeous! exclaimed Romero suddenly. Was she sick? She was dying, he said, and all on her
own like a stray dog, or that's how it looked to me anyway,
after spending two afternoons with her at the clinic, and in
spite of everything she had stayed calm and lucid. She liked
to talk; it was obvious that visitors cheered her up (she didn't
seem to have many, though I couldn't really tell). She was
always reading or writing letters or watching television with
her headphones on. She read news magazines and glossies. Her
room was very tidy and it smelt good. So did she. Before visitors arrived, she probably brushed her hair and dabbed some
cologne or perfume on her neck and hands. I imagine she did,
anyway. The last time I saw her, before we said good-bye, she
turned on the television and switched to something on an
Italian channel. I was worried it might be one of her films.
That really would have been too much for me, I swear. I don't
know what I would have done. But it was a talk show; one of
her old friends was being interviewed. We shook hands and I
left. As I was going out of the door, I couldn't help glancing
back at her. She already had the headphones on, and there was
an odd expression on her face, a military sort of expression, I
don't know how else to describe it, as if her sick room were

the cockpit of a space ship and she were the pilot firmly in control. And what happened in the end? I asked (by this stage I didn't feel like teasing him at all). Nothing. She remembered English and described him for me pretty well, but there would have been thousands of men in Europe fitting the description, and she didn't recognise him in the photo of the pilot, which wasn't surprising, it's more than twenty years old, my friend. I meant, what happened with Joanna Silvestri? She died, said Romero. When? A few months later, when I was back in Paris, I saw the obituary in *Libération*. And you've never seen any of her films? I asked. Joanna Silvestri's? No, of course not. Why would I? Never? You weren't curious? No, I wasn't; I'm a married man and too old for all that, said Romero.

Dinner was on me that night. We ate in the Calle Riera, in a cheap family restaurant, and then we went wandering through the nearby streets. We came to a video library that was open and I told Romero to come with me. You're not going to get one of her films, are you? I heard him say behind me. I don't trust your description, I said, I want to know what she really looked like. There were three shelves of porno films at the back of the premises. I think it was only the second time I had been to a video library. I hadn't felt so good in ages, although there was something burning inside me. It took him a while to find what we were looking for. It was a pleasure just to watch his dark, gnarled hands moving over the spines of the cassettes. Here we go, he said. He was right, she was a very beautiful woman. When we came out, I realized that the video library was the only shop still open in the district.

The next day, when Romero came to my flat, I told him I thought I had identified Wieder. If you saw him again, would you be able to recognise him? I don't know, I replied.

9

This is my last communiqué from the planet of the monsters. Never again will I immerse myself in literature's bottomless cesspools. I will go back to writing my poems, such as they are, find a job to keep body and soul together, and make no attempt to be published.

Among the magazines piled up on my table, two in particular caught my attention. The others could have provided material for a variegated sampler of psychopathy and schizophrenia, but only two had the *élan*, the singularity of purpose that would have attracted Carlos Wieder. Both were French: the first number of the *Evreux Literary Gazette* and No. 3 of the *Arras Nightwatchman's Review.* In both I found critical essays by a certain Jules Defoe, although in the *Gazette* the text was set out, quite arbitrarily, as verse. But first I should say a word about Raoul Delorme and the sect known as "the barbaric writers".

Born in 1935, Raoul Delorme began his working life as a soldier, then sold produce in a wholesale market, before becoming a caretaker in central Paris, a job better suited to someone suffering, as he did, from slight damage to the vertebrae, a souvenir of his time in the Foreign Legion. In 1968, while the students were building barricades and the rising generation of French novelists were putting bricks through the windows of their schools or losing their virginity, he decided to found the sect or movement called "the barbaric writers". While intellectuals were taking to the streets, the ex-legionnaire shut himself up in his tiny caretaker's flat in the Rue des Eaux and began to hatch a new kind of writing. The apprenticeship consisted of two apparently simple steps: seclusion and reading. In order to take the first step, one had to purchase provisions sufficient for a week, or go hungry. To avoid inopportune visits, it was also necessary to make it clear that one was not to be disturbed for any reason, or pretend to be away travelling for a week or to have contracted a contagious disease. The second step was more complicated. According to Delorme, one had to commune with the master works. Communion was achieved in a singularly odd fashion: by defecating on the pages of Stendhal, blowing one's nose on the pages of Victor Hugo, masturbating and spreading one's semen over the pages of Gautier or Banville, vomiting onto the pages of Daudet, urinating on the pages of Lamartine, cutting oneself with a razor blade and spattering blood over the pages of Balzac or Maupassant, in short, submitting the books to a process of degradation which Delorme called "humanisation". A week of these "barbaric" rituals resulted in a flat or room full of filth, stench and ruined books, with the apprentice writer wallowing in the mess, naked or in underwear, drivelling and wriggling like a new-born baby, or, rather, like the pioneering fish that had decided to make the break and live out of water. The barbaric writer, said Delorme, emerged from this experience with a new inner strength, and, more importantly, a deeper understanding of the art of writing, a wisdom acquired through what he called "real familiarity" with and "real assimilation" of the classics, a physical familiarity that broke all the barriers imposed by culture, the academy and technology.

No-one knows how, but he soon acquired a certain following. Like him, his disciples were uneducated and came from humble backgrounds. Beginning in May '68, alone or in groups of two, three or even four, they shut themselves up twice a year in tiny attics, caretakers' flats, hotel rooms, suburban bungalows, the backs of shops and stores in order to prepare the advent of the new literature, a literature that *could* in principle belong to everyone, according to Delorme, but that in practice would only belong to those who dared to cross the bridge of fire. While waiting for the great day, they produced fanzines, which they sold from makeshift stalls, set up wherever they could find a space at the countless second-hand book markets that spring up in squares and streets throughout France. Naturally, most of "the barbaric writers" were poets, although some wrote stories and others experimented with short plays. The titles of their magazines were anodyne or fanciful (there was a list of the movement's publications in the *Evreux Literary Gazette*: the *Inland Seas*, the *Provençal Literary Bulletin*, the *Toulon Review of Arts and Letters*, the *New Literary School* etc.). The *Arras Nightwatchmen's Review* (which was indeed published by a cooperative of nightwatchmen in Arras) provided a

reasonably representative and wide-ranging anthology of barbaric writing. A section entitled "Profession: Amateur" contained
poems by Delorme, Sabrina Martin, Ilse Kraunitz, M. Poul,
Antoine Dubacq and Antoine Madrid, each represented by a
single poem, except for Delorme and Dubacq who had contributed three and two poems respectively. As if to underline
the amateur status of the poets, their day jobs were given in
brackets under their names and beside the odd passport-like
photos, thus informing the reader that Kraunitz was a nursing
aide in a geriatric care unit in Strasbourg, Sabrina Martin
cleaned flats in Paris, and M. Poul worked as a butcher, while
Antoine Madrid and Antoine Dubacq earned their francs selling newspapers from stands on a Paris boulevard. There was
something subtly intriguing about the photos of Delorme and
his band: first, they were all staring into the camera as if engaged
in a childish (or at least futile) attempt to hypnotise the photographer or, through him, the readers; secondly, every one of them
seemed confident and utterly self-assured, immune to ridicule
and doubt, a condition which, on reflection, is perhaps not
altogether exceptional, given that these were French writers. The
differences in age were striking; whatever united the barbaric
writers, it was clearly not the sense of belonging to a generation. There were two generations, at least, between Delorme,
who was more than sixty (although he didn't look it) and
Antoine Madrid, who can't have been more than twenty-two.
In both magazines the texts were preceded by "A History of
Barbaric Writing", signed Xavier Rouberg, and a manifesto by
Delorme himself, entitled "A Passion for Writing". Delorme's

rather pedantic and awkward screed and Rouberg's surprisingly agile and elegant essay (accompanied by a brief note, which he probably wrote himself, presenting the author as an ex-surrealist, ex-communist and ex-fascist, now living in retirement in Poitou, and mentioning, among his works, a book on "his friend" Salvador Dalí, entitled *Dalí and the Opera of the World: Prosecution and Defence*) both recounted the origins of barbaric writing and the milestones that had marked its subterranean and occasionally turbulent evolution. Rouberg and Delorme aside, the others could easily have been mistaken for active (or at least aspiring) members of a writers' group in some working-class suburb. Their faces were ordinary: Sabrina Martin looked thirtyish and cheerless; there was something about Antoine Madrid that suggested the discreet, wary kind of gay, the kind who keeps his distance; Antoine Dubacq was bald, short-sighted and about forty; outwardly Madame Kraunitz could have passed for an office worker of indefinite age, but she seemed to be hiding an immense reserve of unstable energy; M. Poul, around fifty, had a skull-like head, flat ears, a crew-cut, a pointy face, a long, cartilaginous nose and a prominent Adam's apple; as for Delorme, the leader, he looked just like the man he was: a strong willed ex-legionnaire. (But how could *he*, of all people, have imagined that desecrating books was the way to improve one's spoken and written French? At what point in his life did he discover the guiding principle behind this ritual?) The texts signed Xavier Rouberg (whom the editor of the *Arras Nightwatchman's Review* described as the John the Baptist of the new literary movement) were accompanied by contributions from Jules Defoe: an essay in the *Review* and a poem in the *Gazette*. In a jerky and ferocious style, the essay argued that literature should be written by non-literary people, just as politics should be and indeed was being taken over by non-politicians, as the author was delighted to observe. The corresponding revolution in writing, Defoe went on to say, would, in a sense, abolish literature itself. When poetry is written by non-poets and read by non-readers. Any one of them could have written it, I thought. Rouberg perhaps (except for the style, which was totally different: Rouberg, you could tell, was old; once elegant, now he was ironic and venomous, and he was a European – literature, for him, was a navigable river, hazardous admittedly, but a river, not a hurricane, seen far off in an immensity of open space), or Delorme himself (assuming that by eviscerating hundreds of volumes of nineteenth-century French literature he had finally learned how to write prose, which is quite an assumption), or anyone else determined to set the world alight; but something told me this particular champion of barbaric writing was Carlos Wieder.

As to the poem (a narrative poem, which, to my eternal shame, reminded me of John Cage's poetic diary spliced with lines that sounded like Julián del Casal or Magallanes Moure translated into French by a Japanese psychotic), what can I say? It was one of Carlos Wieder's ultimate jokes. And it was deadly serious.

IO

Two months went by before I saw Romero again.

When he came back to Barcelona he was thinner. I've tracked down Jules Defoe, he said. You know, all this time he's been living practically next door. How about that, eh? Romero's smile frightened me.

He was thinner and he looked like a dog. Let's go, he said crisply that afternoon. He left his suitcase in my flat and as we went out he made sure I locked the door. All I had time to say was: I wasn't expecting it all to happen so quickly. Romero was already in the hall. He looked at me and said, We have to go on a little trip, I'll explain on the way. Have we really found him? I asked. I don't know why I used the plural. We've found Jules Defoe, he replied, with a movement of the head that could have meant almost anything. I followed him like a sleepwalker.

It must have been months, or maybe even years, since I had ventured out of Barcelona, and the Plaza Cataluña station, just a few blocks from my apartment, looked completely unfamiliar: brightly lit and full of new contraptions installed for purposes mysterious to me. On my own I would never have been able to proceed with Romero's briskness and efficiency, and having noticed or foreseen my predictable bewilderment, he took it on himself to guide me through the devices blocking access to the platforms. Then, after waiting a few minutes in silence, we took the local train that runs along the edge of the Maresme and over the River Tordera to Blanes, where the Costa Brava begins. As we were leaving Barcelona, I asked him who his client was. A Chilean, said Romero. We went through two métro stations, then emerged into the suburbs. Suddenly the sea appeared. A weak sun lit the beaches, which flashed past like the beads of a necklace suspended not from a neck but in empty space. A Chilean? And what's in it for him? You're better off not knowing, said Romero, but you can guess. Is he paying a lot? (If he is, I thought, this can only be leading to one thing.) A fair bit; he's made a fortune in the last few years, sighed Romero, and in Chile too, not abroad. How about that? Apparently quite a few people are getting rich in Chile these days. So I've heard, I said, in what was meant to be a sarcastic tone of voice, but it probably just sounded sad. And what are you going to do with the money? Are you thinking of going back to Chile? Yes, I'm going back, said Romero. After a while he added, I've got a plan, an idea. I've been working it out in Paris and it can't go wrong. And what's your plan? I asked. A business, he said. I'm going to set up my own business. I didn't react. Every exiled Chilean was planning to go back and set up a business. Looking out of the window of the train, I saw a magnificent modernist house with a tall palm tree in the garden. I'm going to become a funeral director, said Romero. I'll start small, but I'm confident the business will grow. I thought he was joking. Stop pulling my leg, I said. I'm serious. The secret is to provide a decent funeral for people who don't have much money, something dignified, even elegant (this is where the French are unbeatable): high-class touches for the middle class, a middle-class service for the working class. That's the key to success, not just in the undertaking business, but in life in general! Knowing how to treat the family of the deceased, commenting on how kind, courteous and morally superior the stiff was, whoever it happened to be. Three rooms, he said as the train pulled out of Badalona and I began to realise that this was for real and that it was too late to turn back, three well-furnished rooms will be enough for a start: one for the office and tidying up the bodies, one for the wakes, and a waiting room with armchairs and ashtrays. Ideally I'd like to rent a little two-storey house somewhere central, live upstairs and use the ground floor for the funeral parlour. It'll be a family business; my wife and son can help out (although I'm not so sure about my son), but I'm thinking it would be good to hire a secretary too, a quiet, hard-working sort of girl. As you know, at wakes and funerals people really appreciate the physical presence of the young. Naturally, every now and then, the boss (or in his absence, an assistant) has to come out and offer the friends and relatives a drink, pisco or whatever. This has to be done in a sympathetic and tactful manner. Without pretending that you were close to the deceased, but making it clear that you understand what they're going through. It's important to talk softly and not be over-eager. When shaking hands, you take the other person's elbow in your left hand. You have to know whom to kiss and when, and how to join in the conversations, whatever the subject – politics, football, life in general or the seven deadly sins – without taking sides, like a retired judge. The profit on the coffins can be as much as three hundred per cent. I have an old friend in Santiago from my homicide days who's gone in for making chairs. I was telling him about my idea the other day on the phone and he said, Chairs, coffins, it's all woodwork. I could make do for the first year with a black station wagon. You have to remember it's mainly about knowing how to deal with people, not elbow grease. And having lived abroad for years, I've got plenty of stories to tell . . . People in Chile are dying to hear stuff like that.

But I had stopped listening to Romero. I was thinking of Bibiano O'Ryan, Marta Posadas, and the sea staring me in the face. For a moment I imagined Fat Marta working in a hospital in Concepción, married and reasonably happy. Unwittingly, unwillingly she had been the devil's intimate, but she was alive. I imagined her with children, still a keen reader, but prudent and balanced in her choices. Then I thought of Bibiano O'Ryan, who had stayed in Chile and followed Wieder's tracks. I saw him working in the shoe shop, helping doubtful-looking middle-aged women try on high-heeled shoes, or serving innocuous children, with a shoe-horn in one hand and a sad-looking Bata shoebox in the other, smiling absently, day after day, until he reached the age of thirty-three, just like Jesus Christ, and then I saw him publishing successful books, signing copies at the Santiago Book Fair (if such a thing exists) and spending semesters as visiting professor at North American universities, whimsically deciding to lecture on the new Chilean poetry or contemporary Chilean poetry (whimsically, because the serious choice would have been the novel) and mentioning me, albeit near the end of his list, out of sheer loyalty or pity: An odd sort of poet, working, last I heard, in a factory somewhere in Europe . . . I saw him climbing like a sherpa towards the peak of his career, winning respect, status and wealth, perfectly placed to settle his scores with the past. I don't know what it was that possessed me: melancholy, nostalgia or justifiable envy (which in Chile, by the way, is often the cruellest kind), but for a moment I thought that Bibiano might have hired Romero. I said so. No, it's not your friend, Romero said. He wouldn't have enough money to get me started. My client, he said, lowering his voice and adopting a falsely confidential tone, is someone who has *real* money, if you see what I mean. Of course, I said, and he didn't make it from writing. Romero smiled to himself. Look at the sea, he said. Look at the countryside. Beautiful, isn't it? I looked out of the window: on one side the sea looked as calm as a millpond; on the other, in the orchards of the Maresme, black men were labouring.

The train stopped in Blanes. Romero said something I didn't catch and we got off. I felt as if I had cramp in my legs. Outside the station, in the little square that seemed round although it was in fact square, a red bus and a yellow bus were parked. Romero bought some chewing gum. Noticing how drawn I looked and hoping to cheer me up, I suppose, he asked which bus I thought we were going to take. The red one, I said. Right you are, said Romero.

The bus dropped us off in Lloret. It was the middle of a dry spring and there were not many tourists around. We took a street that led downhill, then one that climbed steeply and another that brought us to a district full of holiday flats, most of them unoccupied. The silence was strange, intensified by faint animal noises, as if there were a field or a farm nearby. In one of the soulless buildings surrounding us lived Carlos Wieder.

How did I end up here? I thought. How many streets did I have to walk to end up on this one?

During the train journey I had asked Romero if it had been hard to find Delorme. No, he said, it was simple. He was still working in Paris as a caretaker, and treated every visitor as a potential source of publicity. I pretended to be a journalist, said Romero. And did he believe you? Of course he did. I told him I was planning to publish the complete history of the barbaric writers in a Colombian newspaper. Delorme was in Lloret last summer. In fact, the apartment where Defoe is staying belongs to one of his disciples. Poor Defoe, I said. Romero looked at me as if I'd gone mad. I don't feel sorry for people like that, he said. By then we had reached the building: tall, wide, devoid of style, a typical product of the tourist boom, with empty balconies and an anonymous, neglected façade. I couldn't imagine anyone living in it, or perhaps just a few sad cases left over from last summer. I wanted to know what was going to happen to Wieder. Romero didn't answer my question. I don't want anyone to get hurt, I murmured, as if someone else could hear me, although we were the only two people in the street. I couldn't look at Romero or at Wieder's building; I felt I was trapped in a recurring nightmare. When I wake up, I thought, my mother will make me a mortadella sandwich and I'll go off to school. But I wasn't going to wake up. This is where he lives, said Romero. The building and the whole district were empty, waiting for the start of the next tourist season. For a moment I thought we were going in and I hung back. Keep walking, said Romero. His voice sounded calm, like the voice of a man who knows that in real life things always turn out badly and there's no point getting worked up about it. I felt his hand brush against my elbow. Keep going straight ahead, he said, and don't look back. We must have been an odd sight, the pair of us.

The building resembled a fossilised bird. For a moment I had the impression that Carlos Wieder's eyes were watching me from every window. I'm getting really nervous, I said to Romero. Does it show? No, my friend, he replied, you're doing well. Romero was quite unruffled and that helped me to calm down. A few streets further on we stopped at the door of a bar, which seemed to be the only place open in the area. It had an Andalusian name and the décor was a rather sad attempt to reproduce the atmosphere of a typical Seville *taberna*. Romero came to the door with me. He looked at his watch. He'll come here for a coffee in a while, I can't say when exactly. And what if he doesn't turn up? I know for sure he comes every day, said Romero, and he'll come today. But what if, for some reason, he doesn't? Well, then we'll come back tomorrow, said Romero, but he'll come, don't you worry. I nodded. Have a good look at him and then you can tell me. Take a seat and don't move.

It might be hard not to move, I said. Do your best. I smiled at him. I was only joking, I said. Must be your nerves, said Romero. I'll come back when it gets dark. Rather too firmly and solemnly, we shook hands. Have you brought something to read? Yes, I said. What is it? I showed him. Hmm, I don't know if it's a good choice, said Romero, with a dubious expression. A magazine or a newspaper might have been better. Don't worry, I said, this is a writer I like a lot. Romero looked at me one last time and said, See you soon, and remember, it's more than twenty years ago now.

From the front windows of the bar there was a view of the sea, with a few fishing boats at work near the coast, under an intensely blue sky. I ordered a coffee with milk and tried to calm down; I felt as if my heart was going to burst out of my chest. The bar was almost empty. There was a woman sitting at a table reading a magazine and two men talking or arguing with the bartender. I opened the book, the *Complete Works of Bruno Schulz*, translated by Juan Carlos Vidal, and tried to read. After a few pages I realised I wasn't understanding anything. I was reading, but the words went scuttling past like beetles, busy at incomprehensible tasks. I thought of Bibiano again, and Fat Marta. I didn't want to think about the Garmendia sisters, so distant now, or the other women, but I couldn't help myself.

Nobody came into the bar; nobody moved. Time seemed to be standing still. I started to feel sick; the fishing boats on the sea had turned into yachts (so there must be wind, I thought). The coast was uniformly grey and every once in a while someone walked or cycled past on the broad, empty pavement. I estimated that it would take about five minutes to get to the beach. It was downhill all the way.

There was hardly a cloud in the sky. An ideal sky, I thought.

Then Carlos Wieder came in and sat down by the front window, three tables away. For a nauseating moment I could see myself almost joined to him, like a vile Siamese twin, looking over his shoulder at the book he had opened (a scientific book, about the greenhouse effect or the origin of the universe), so close he couldn't fail to notice, but, as Romero had predicted, Wieder didn't recognise me.

He had aged. Like me, I suppose. But no, much more than me. He was fatter, more wrinkled; he looked at least ten years older than I did, although in fact there was a difference of only two or three years. He was staring at the sea and smoking and glancing at his book every now and then. Just like me, I realised with a fright, stubbing out my cigarette and trying to merge into the pages of my book. But Bruno Schulz's words had momentarily taken on a monstrous character that was almost intolerable. I felt that Wieder's lifeless eyes were scrutinising me, while the letters on the pages I was turning (perhaps too quickly) were no longer beetles but eyes, the eyes of Bruno Schulz, opening and closing, over and over, eyes pale as the sky, shining like the surface of the sea, opening, blinking, again and again, in the midst of total darkness. No, not total, in the midst of a milky darkness, like the inside of a storm cloud.

When I looked again at Carlos Wieder, he had turned side on. It struck me that he had a hard look peculiar to certain Latin Americans over the age of forty, quite different from the hardness you see in Europeans or North Americans. A sad, irreparable sort of hardness. But Carlos Wieder (who had won the heart of at least one of the Garmendia sisters) did not appear to be sad and that is precisely where the infinite sadness lay. He seemed *adult*. But he wasn't adult, I knew that straightaway. He seemed self-possessed. And in his own way, on his own terms, whatever they were, he was more self-possessed than the rest of us in that sleepy bar, or most of the people walking by on the beach or invisibly at work, getting ready for the imminent tourist season. He was hard, he had nothing or very little and it didn't seem to bother him much. He seemed to be going through a rough patch. He had the face of a man who knows how to wait without losing his nerve or letting his imagination run wild. He didn't look like a poet. He didn't look as if he had been an officer in the Chilean Air Force. He didn't look like an infamous killer. He didn't look like a man who had flown to Antarctica to write a poem in the sky. Not at all.

As it was starting to get dark, he rummaged in his pocket for a coin, left it on the table by way of a meagre tip, got up and went out. The door was behind me; when I heard it swing shut, I didn't know whether to burst out laughing or crying. I sighed with relief. The feeling of freedom, of having finally solved a problem, was so intense I was worried the others would read it on my face. The two men were still at the bar, talking quietly (not arguing at all), as if they had all the time in the world. A cigarette hung from the bartender's lips as he watched the woman, who now and then looked up from her magazine and smiled at him. She must have been around thirty and her profile was striking. Deep in thought, she looked somehow Greek, or as if she'd been Greek in another life. Suddenly I felt light-hearted and hungry. I caught the bartender's eye and ordered a ham roll and a beer. When he brought them out we exchanged a few words. I tried to go on reading, but I couldn't, so I just sat there, eating, drinking and looking out of the window at the sea, while I waited for Romero.

He arrived shortly and we left together. At first we seemed to be going away from Wieder's building, but in fact we were just circling around it. Is it him? asked Romero. Yes, I said. Are you certain? I'm certain. I was going to say something more, launch into ethical and aesthetic reflections on the passing of time (stupidly, since as far as Wieder was concerned, time meant nothing more than erosion), but Romero quickened his pace. He has a job to do, I thought. *We* have a job to do, I realised, horrified. We made our way through streets and alleys until Wieder's building loomed on the horizon, lit by the moon. It was somehow different from the buildings around it, which seemed to be shrinking away or losing definition, as if it had cast a spell or were repelling them with its concentrated solitude.

Romero steered me into a small park, full of plants like a botanical garden. He pointed to a bench almost hidden by the branches. Wait for me here, he said. I sat down obediently. I was trying to make out his face in the darkness. Are you going to kill him? I murmured. Romero gestured in reply, but it was too dark to see what he meant. Wait for me here or go to the station in Blanes and catch the first train. We'll see each other back in Barcelona. It's not a good idea, I said. It could ruin our lives, yours and mine, and anyway what's the point? He's not going to do any more harm now. It's not going to ruin *my* life, said Romero. Quite the opposite; it's going to set me up. And as to whether he'll do any more harm, all I can say is: we don't know, we can't know; you're not God and nor am I; we're only doing what we can, that's all. I couldn't see his face, but I could tell by the voice emanating from his rock-still silhouette that he was making an effort to be convincing. It's not worth it, I persisted. It's over now. No-one needs to get hurt now. Romero slapped me on the shoulder. Better you stay out of this, he said. I'll be back soon.

As his footfalls grew fainter, I sat there watching the dark shrubs, their tangled branches weaving random designs as they shifted in the wind. Then I lit a cigarette and began to think about trivial matters. Like time. The greenhouse effect. The increasingly distant stars.

I tried to think of Wieder. I tried to imagine him alone in his flat, an anonymous dwelling, as I pictured it, on the fourth floor of an empty eight-floor building, watching television or sitting in an armchair, drinking, as Romero's shadow glided steadily towards him. I tried to imagine Carlos Wieder, but I couldn't. Or maybe I didn't really want to.

Half an hour later Romero returned, with a folder under his arm, one of those folders that kids take to school, with elastic bands to hold it closed. It was bulging with papers, but could have held more. It was green, like the shrubs in the park, and worn. That was all. Romero didn't seem any different. He didn't seem better or worse than before. He was breathing easily. As

I looked at him it struck me that he was the spitting image of Edward G. Robinson. If you can imagine Edward G. Robinson put through a meat grinder and slightly rearranged: thinner, with darker skin and more hair, but the same lips, the same nose and above all the same knowing eyes. Eyes ready to believe that anything is possible but *knowing*, too, that nothing can be undone. Let's go, he said.

We took the bus from Lloret back to Blanes and then the train to Barcelona. Along the way Romero made a couple of attempts to start a conversation. He praised the "boldly modern" design of Spanish trains. He said what a pity it was he wouldn't be able to see Barcelona play at the Nou Camp. I said nothing or replied with monosyllables. I didn't feel like talking. I remember it was a beautiful, calm night outside. Groups of boys and girls kept getting on at one station and off at the next, as if it were a game. They were probably going to local discos: less expensive and closer to home. All of them were under eighteen and some had the look of young heroes. They seemed to be happy. Later we stopped in a bigger station and a group of workers who could have been their parents got on. And later still, but I'm not sure when, we went through various tunnels and one of the girls shrieked when the lights in the compartment went out. When they came on again, I looked at Romero's face; it was the same as ever. Finally, when we arrived at the Plaza Cataluña station, we began to talk. I asked him what it had been like. Like these things always are, he said. Difficult.

We walked back to my flat. When we got there, he opened his suitcase, took out an envelope and handed it to me. In the envelope were three hundred thousand pesetas. I don't need this much money, I said after counting it. It's yours, said Romero, as he packed the folder in his case with his clothes and shut it. You've earned it. I haven't earned anything, I said. Instead of replying, Romero went into the kitchen and put the kettle on. Where will you be going? I asked him. Paris, he said. I've got a flight at midnight; I want to sleep in my own bed tonight. We had a last cup of tea together and I went down to the street with him. We stood there for a while on the edge of the pavement waiting for a taxi, not knowing what to say. Nothing like this has ever happened to me, I confessed. That's not true, said Romero very gently. Worse things have happened to us, think about it. You could be right, I admitted, but this really has been a dreadful business. Dreadful, repeated Romero, as if he were savouring the word. Then he laughed quietly, grinning like a rabbit, and said, Well, what else could it have been? I wasn't in a laughing mood, but I laughed all the same. Romero looked at the sky, the lighted windows, the car headlights, the neon signs, and he seemed small and tired. Soon, I guessed, he would be sixty. And I had already passed forty. A taxi pulled up beside us. Look after yourself, my friend, he said, and off he went.